Ken Lansdowne

HOME SWEET Ho Mo

A Bent Mystery

4

H Publishing

Dedicated To:
Dick Neibaur
Who, one night, out of the blue,
made an offer that changed my life.
I'll always be grateful.

Copyright © 2012 by Ken Lansdowne.
Publisher: H Publishing
605 Clinton Street,
Denver, Colorado 80247.

PUBLISHERS NOTE: This is a work of
fiction. Names, characters, places, and
incidents are the product of the authors
imagination or are used fictitiously. Any
resemblance to actual persons living or
dead, events or locals are entirely coin-
cidental.

First Printing: 2012

Library of Congress Cataloging in Publication Data
    Home sweet homo: a bent mystery: a novel/ Ken Lansd-
owne
        p. cm.
    ISBN 0-9740853-1-6/978-0-9740853-1-9
    1. Title

Printed in USA   H Publishing

OTHER BOOKS BY THE AUTHOR

HOME SWEET *Ho Mo*

Foreward

It was almost ten at night. A police car was sitting in the dark under the bridge, along with a swarm of mosquito's attracted to a fetid puddle of rainwater that muddied the ground. An owl sat looking down from a tree outside the concrete structure. He had been around long enough to have seen everything and a parked cop car wasn't anything new for him. He asked his usual question and let it go.

The dark was only occasionally disturbed by the glow from a cigarette smoked by the cop sitting in the vehicle. His name was Vince Barkley. He was a member of the Peebles Police Force in Peebles, Kansas, which was located about eighty-five miles outside Wichita. He waited expectantly. It had been twenty-five minutes he'd been sitting. He didn't mind all that much. Hell, he got paid for the time. If anyone asked, he was using his radar to catch speeders. As if there might be a speeder out on this Godforsaken road. That was the beauty of it. Being out where nobody could see him while the best cocksucker in the county was going down on him. Where the hell was that cocksucker anyway?

Vince sat alone for a few more minutes, until the lights from another car illuminated his back-end as it pulled up. It's about fricking time, he thought. Now we can get it on. He rubbed his hands together in anticipation.

The second car's lights went out. For a moment Vince couldn't see. Until his eyes got used to the dark of the night again. When they had adjusted, he looked out his side window. Standing there was his expected guest.

"It's about time," Vince said as he rolled down the glass. "I've been looking forward to this all day." The man at the window went over to the passenger side, pulled open the door, and started to get in.

"Don't get too comfortable there. I'm coming over." Vince got out of his side and walked around, while the other man stood by the open door. When Vince was over on that side he grabbed the man roughly and pulled him close. They kissed. When he was finished Vince let the man go, then said, "Here's the key. The stuff's in the trunk."

The man took the keys from him and went to the back of the car. He looked in the trunk and took out a coil of spun nylon rope, a couple of beach towels, and a paper bag of other supplies Vince had stored there. He went back to the door. It took him only a moment to unfold one of the towels and drape it over the passenger seat of the cops car.

Vince smiled, "Thanks. Gotta keep the upholstery clean, right?" He sat down on the car seat with his legs out, his feet on the ground. He reached for the rope and took it from the man. "I'm sorry, lover," he said. "We gotta hurry tonight. I got someone coming to meet me at eleven."

Vince took the rope and loosened its coils. Next he found the end and tied a quick slip knot. With practiced turns Vince wound the rope around his own neck, put the end through the knot, and handed the rest of the rope back to the man. He turned in the seat and faced front. He could see the owl's eyes shining in the dark out the front window. Vince's hand rubbed at his crotch in anticipation of what was to come.

The man hung the rope over the back of the seat, and let it fall loose to the rear floorboards. Then he stuffed the rope under the seat until he could grab hold of it at the front. Once he had the rope again Vince held out his wrists as if he was waiting to have a pair of handcuffs put on. The man wrapped the cord a couple of turns around Vince's wrists and tied it off. Then the man climbed over Vince's knees into the hole under the dash. Facing toward him he unzipped Vince's trousers.

"Hey," Vince said. "Remember?"

The man reached into the paper bag and grabbed a tube of lipstick. Crafty Crimson. He pulled off the top and smeared the red goo on his mouth.

"God," Vince said, taking a deep breath, "even the smell of that stuff turns me on. Look, it made me hard already, and you ain't even touched me yet."

The man reached forward and took hold of Vince's cock. He licked his lips, leaned his head forward, and went down on him. Vince laid his head back on the car seat headrest and moaned. "That's it, baby. Suck it good."

As the blowjob progressed Vince would use his tied wrists to pull up on the rope; that would in turn put pressure on his neck, heightening for him the feeling of the sucking mouth on his dick.

As the two men got into the rhythm of their sex act Vince would pull harder on the rope, losing himself in the wet sucking feeling that would again and again bring him close to his climax. Then by letting the pressure on the rope go slack he could prolong his pleasure. Over and over Vince brought himself close to cumming. "Suck it, you son of a bitch. Take it," he would shout, then force his hips against the man's face, grinding his pelvis into the man's throat.

Lost in his mounting ecstasy Vince didn't notice when the man reached up and took hold of his tied hands. It was passion, after all. The man got a hard grip on Vince's hands, then began to push up. He pushed Vince's trussed hands further toward his head. In essence, he was doing to Vince what Vince had been doing to himself. Vince, feeling only his own pleasure, even egged him on. "Yeah, baby, make it good."

But the man's intention wasn't passion.

The man continued to push up on Vince's arms. Then he took his mouth off Vince's member, leaving it throbbing at his crotch. The man rose in the confined space and pressed harder on Vince's arms. Pushing upward, using all his weight, forcing Vince's arms even farther over his head.

Vince, realizing that he couldn't breathe, started to struggle. His body stiffened as he frantically tried to indicate to the man to loosen the rope that was choking him. The man didn't. Wouldn't. Instead, he pushed more, and kept pushing. Pushing until Vince's arms were stretched out above his head. Vince fought to stay alive, writhing and twisting in the car seat.

Then Vince twisted less. And less. Finally, Vince's head lolled off to the side, his tongue hanging out like a schnauzer's on a hot day. Vince stared with bulging eyes at his killer as he died.

The last thing Vince saw was the red lipstick smudged over the man's chin.

The man, finished, climbed over the body and got out of the car. Using the towel he had left on the car's roof he wiped at his mouth. Then he bent in and opened the glove compartment of the police car. A quick rummage and he stood back up. He was holding a black pocketbook sized notepad. He flipped the pages until he got to the last one written on. He tore that page out, folded it, and stuck it in his shirt pocket, then chucked the notebook back into the cars interior.

He walked to his own car, sat behind the steering wheel and grabbed a cigarette from the pack stashed in the gear box slot. After a few drags he crushed it out, turned the key in the ignition, and pulled back. The cop car and its now dead passenger faded into the darkness as he drove away.

The owl spotted a field mouse scurrying across the dirt road below him. He flew down for a late snack. His third meal of the day. Life was good.

Notes From Home

"But, JB, I don't know why she won't talk. She refuses to say. You know how she is?"

Sara, JB's sister, had just told him that his mother refused to speak with him. He was making his usual monthly call back to his hometown in Kansas.

"Well," JB said. "its one more dustup isn't it? You know our whole relationship has been like this ever since I came out. We didn't talk for almost a year after that. And that was twenty years ago. So, I'll get along without talking to her this week. Now, tell me what's going on there in town?"

"Oh, I've got to tell you about Howard. His sister asked me too. He's been arrested, JB. I know it sounds crazy, but the police chief has him in jail on some trumped up drug charges?"

"Well, that's stupid. Howard never took drugs. Even when we were kids." Howard Fellows was JB's oldest friend. They had lived in houses behind each other since Howard was three and a half. JB had been already four. Howard's father had made a fortune in the stock market so they lived in a huge old place one street over from JB's. Big and spooky, it was a mansion in the Victorian style with an enormous backyard. There was even a tiny peach orchard, five trees, that separated their houses. JB and his family lived in a smaller one-family with a backyard that faced Howard's. They hadn't become real friends until they were about five. They got sent to school together. Safety in numbers their Mom's figured.

"No, not for using, Older Brother," Sara said. "For selling. The Chief claims he was mixed up with a group of drug dealers."

"If he was it was because he was after a story." Howard was the star newspaper reporter in JB's old hometown. Actually he was the only newspaper reporter in JB's hometown. But he had ambitions. Howard was looking to get out of Peebels, Kansas and move over to the next big city—Wichita. Howard saw that as an upward move. JB thought of it as more lateral.

"But there's more," Sara added. "The Chief also wants to charge him with a murder. One of their cops was killed the other night, and they're trying to blame Howard. His sister was hoping you might help."

"I can't, Sara. I'm up against a huge deadline here. I have to get my proofed galleys back to my publisher in less than two weeks, and I have to correct the entire set." JB was a successful writer of murder mystery's. His latest book would be published in the winter by Kipling, his small press publisher. It's story concerned catching the Fairy Dust Killer. JB had been involved in his capture several months before, and had used the situation as a basis for his latest book. Sort of a real-life novel. Like Truman Capote had done when he wrote *In Cold Blood.*

"JB, you know darn well that you could bring those galleys with you when you come home. You have to. Howard was only your best friend ever."

She was right. Howard Fellows and JB had a very close friendship when they were boys. Quite frankly, as a child JB had worshiped him. Howard was everything JB had wanted to be. Handsome, popular, athletic, talented. The list went on.

Howard had put out his first newspaper when he was seven. JB helped. Howard said he was going to be a newspaper man, like Clark Kent. Not Superman, mind you. But the guy Lois Lane thought was a total wimp. JB got to be Howard's Jimmy Olsen. Howard and JB were investigative reporters for three whole issues. Until they ran a headline that Mrs. Gorden, the neighbor two doors down, was seen stealing pork chops from the local *Piggly-Wiggly.* That scandalized the whole neighborhood and the paper was closed down pronto.

JB sighed. "I guess you're right, Younger Sister. All right, I'll come home. But, I'm staying at the hotel. Not at the house."

"That's my Older Brother. Stubborn. The same as his mother."

And that's how JB ended up later that evening on the subway headed to Penn Station to catch the shuttle out to Kennedy Airport. It was a pain in the tuchus to accomplish when you had a suitcase, a shoulder bag, and a camera in tow. But it was also only seven dollars for the trip, as compared to forty dollars for a cab. JB was successful, not rich, as subjective as that term could be. Success was something that each person had to figure out on his own, at least to what each person thought it was for himself. JB wasn't a Leona Helmsley but who wanted to be her? He bet there were times that even she didn't want to be her, especially when the peons tried to breach the gates of the Palace Hotel. He made a good living there in his town. But his town was New York City. The second most expensive city in the entire world. He'd lived there for a little more than twenty years, and he'd done all right. He owned an interest in the apartment building he lived in. He had his writing career. He had a part interest in a bar and theatre down in the Village, and he possessed a genuine Lautrec sketch. Worth about five or six thousand on the open market. But, JB wasn't extravagant when he was using his own dime. If he was on a book tour it was one thing, then it was his publisher's money. When he had to pay from his own pocket, he tended toward thrifty. A penny for a rainy day? One of the rock-solid tenets taught by Kansas natives from the Founding Fathers on up.

Once out at the airport, after picking up his ticket, he waited for thirty minutes and then caught a direct flight to Chicago. Once there he had to wait another two hours for a connecting flight to get him to Topeka. Then onto a smaller plane that got him to Wichita at about eight the next morning. He called his sister first thing. She offered to drive over from Peebels and pick him up.

He waited for her.

Notes From The Road

The pirate galleon, made to an exact three quarter scale of the real thing, floated over the audience on nearly invisible wires from the second balcony down to the orchestra pit where it hovered over a set representing the top bedroom Victorian London window of the Darling household. A gangplank was slid out and the boy playing Sneed crept across it to Wendy Darlings open window. He went inside and a few seconds later he came back out with the struggling body of the girl, a bag to the waist over her head, slung over his shoulder. He made his way back across the plank to the ship with his wiggling package. As he was about to step onto the deck of the ship, there was a crack of wood and the gangplank fell away from the two of them and down into the pit under them. Thinking quickly, Sneed grabbed one of the ropes swaged on the ship rails and managed to stay swinging on the side of the ship. The audience, not knowing it wasn't supposed to happen, laughed at his predicament, and Sneed, not knowing what to do in said predicament, shouted a loud, and apparently hilarious, "Help" from his position. The girl, still covered with that bag over her head, wasn't aware of their precarious position, but yelped when their bodies swung and smashed against the side of the ship. She stayed lying over his shoulder but was crying loudly from an injury to her shoulder. Her crying was Sneed's only concern at first, then he became aware again of the thousand or so people watching this accident happen in scene 2 of Act 1 of *Hook and Wendy*. What the hell was he supposed to do? The play couldn't stop. Could it? He shouted again, his eyes questioning, looking for anyone to help.

Len Matthews, standing backstage in his costume, the Restoration foppery of Captain Hook himself, immediately ran out to the boat's entrance (a doorway onto the ship hidden from the audience) stage side, and yelled, in character, "Sneed! What's going on here? Where is she?" He moved inside the ship, climbed the few steps up to the deck and leaned over the rail, "Stop playing with your cargo and hand the wench here, Sneed." He bent over and grabbed the girl at the waist, pulled her away from Sneed and into his arms on the deck. "You've got to be more careful, Sneed, my boy. You had precious luggage here. Now, be careful of that dastardly croc." Len twirled his pencil thin mustache, "there are reports he's been in the neighborhood." Len, taking the girl with him, left Sneed to fend for himself. Or more precisely, to drop the few feet into the orchestra pit below him.

The stage went dark.

Once backstage Len sat the girl down in a chair, removed the bag, and bent to examine her shoulder. She gasped as he touched it feeling for a break. There didn't seem to be one, but the amount of pain she evidenced indicated there was something decidedily wrong there. He told one of the onlookers to call an ambulance right away.

Meanwhile, the director had found Wendy's understudy and was getting her dressed, so she could take over the part. The character appeared in the very next scene and they had no time to dawdle. The new girl was costumed and on stage in less than five minutes. Injured Wendy was put on a gurney by the medics that had by then arrived and was rolled off to their vehicle.

The show, of course, according to tradition, continued on. There was only a minutes delay, so the audience wasn't even aware that pandemonium had reigned backstage in those few minutes, or that there was another Wendy in the next scene. Original Wendy was rushed to the nearest hospital to have her shoulder attended to.

During scene 7, while the new Wendy sang of her distress over her kidnapping, Len made his way to the prop ship and inspected the damaged plank. He looked closely at the broken end, still dangling off the ship, and was surprised to discover that the wood hadn't broken because it was rotten. It had been sawed through with a blade enough so that when the weight of both Sneed and the girl was put on the plank it would give way. This hadn't been an accident, Len realized. Someone had deliberately wanted the girl playing Wendy to fall and hurt herself. What a sneaky, meanspirited, and dastardly act on somebody's part. And that was the fifth or sixth "accident" on the show so far. What was going on?

Len couldn't linger over what this latest bit of sabotage signified, he was to appear in scene 9 with Wendy and Sneed, and had to be on stage in just a moment. He ran to his center stage mark as the curtain opened on the scene.

The play went on.

After the show that night, Len got on the phone in his hotel room and tried to call his friend JB.

JB—that would be novelist Jeremy Bent—was his best friend. They had worked together on several projects, even collaborating on one or two cases that JB had gotten them involved in. This wrinkle happening in Len's play would interest him he knew. Len wanted to talk it over with him, get JB's input, before he went to the director and told him what he had discovered concerning that sawed plank.

When the line was connected he got JB's answering machine. Len hated the damn thing. His message was typical smartass JB. He would have to erase it when he got home. That would be simple enough, since Len lived in the same building. They often spent time together watching TV and such. An accidental push on the erase button would be easy to explain.

So JB wasn't at home? Len checked his watch. It was 1 AM back there, only 10 PM where he was. JB was usually working at his writing by this time. If he'd picked up the phone he would have been pissed that Len had disturbed him, but he would have talked. Of course, there were a hundred reasons why JB might not have been at home, but any one of them would have been out of character for JB. He was uber-responsible about his writing and deadlines. Len knew he was facing such a deadline on his current book. So where was he? Len decided he would have to try calling tomorrow during the daytime, JB was more likely to be at home then.

Notes From Home

Checking into the only hotel in Peebels, Kansas was to experience homophobia at its finest. The desk clerk asked JB if he needed a bellhop to carry his purse.

What JB carried was a briefcase with a strap to hold his supplies. Plus the manuscript and a set of galleys for his book. And if truth be known, a couple of leftover fruit rolls from the lunch he had brought along on the plane ride. Airplane food was like toy food. It had little substance and wouldn't satisfy a gnat's appetite.

The clerk, whose nametag identified him as Corey, obviously couldn't imagine a man carrying a shoulder bag. The only term he could find that would explain it was a woman's accessory. Typical of a small town, JB thought to himself. Shoulder bags had been necessary and acceptable in New York for years and years. He should have used the leather backpack he usually carried around New York. That wouldn't have caused the condescending remark, now would it?.

Then the clerk asked him how things were going, and used his first name, Jeremy. He'd been called JB by about everyone since his senior year in high school. His proper name, Jeremy, was only used on book covers and publicity releases. Jere my Bent. Hence, JB. The use of his proper name meant he had to know this man. After a few questions it turned out JB had gone to two years of high school with him. He had only vaguely known him then since Corey was a year behind JB's class, but, once prodded, JB did remember him. As JB went to the elevator he heard Corey say, "Welcome back home, Jeremy."

JB replied with utter confidence. "Just visiting." That was to be taken as gospel as far as he was concerned.

Peebels, Kansas was a small enough town that running into someone he knew when he was younger was more than likely. It was inevitable. JB's high school graduating class was under two hundred, and the majority of them had stayed there in the small town after. But a minority had headed away from Peebels as quick as their little asses could get them to the city limits. That's when JB had fled to New York—immediately after high school.

The day after graduation he was packed and withdrawing his savings from the local bank. Then he had told a few close people that he was gay, just in case they hadn't already figured it out. He'd told his family first, and then, of course, Howard. Howard and JB had remained friends even into high school. Not as close mind you. They tended to run in different circles. Howard was with the popular kids. JB was with the choir nerds, theatre geeks, and yearbook dweebs that every high school was populated with. Howard had been convinced by others it wasn't cool to be seen hanging out with JB. So the friendship had drifted, and they only saw each other occasionally.

At graduation JB held secret hopes Howard would come out to him, declare his everlasting love, and the two of them would move to the big city to create a gay life together. That wasn't how it worked out. Howard did come out to JB. Then begged him not to mention it to anyone. Howard was going to stay in Peebels and in the closet. That closet thing was something JB had decided he couldn't do for himself. Howard had also said he couldn't leave with JB because he'd already been hired on at the local newspaper—it was the first rung on the ladder of Howard's adult life. JB had wondered how the guy was going to manage as a homosexual in small town Peebels. It was a town that if it had any gay life at all, it, with a few exceptions, remained strictly under the surface.

Outwardly, the town despised gay people. It was known to have hounded at least one gay teacher and a choral director out of their chosen professions in the last 20 years. God forbid *they* should teach *their* lifestyle to *their* children. Like in every small town there were one or two gay people that lived there, but they were glaring exceptions. The church organist. A hairdresser at the local salon. They were looked on by the ladies of the town as pets. The perfect extra man for dinner parties. The men of Peebles could bearly manage to tolerate them. And there were no lesbians—a gay woman? Inconceivable.

So Howard, and JB, had been gay boys in a small town. But they'd lucked out and hadn't had it held against them to any great degree. They weren't riden out of town on a rail or tared and feathered by the local gang of toughs. Or bullied beyond some basic name calling. As long as they kept their proclivities private and in the closet it was okay. Neither of them swished— well, maybe JB did some. Enough that it wasn't a surprise to anyone when he did finally came out.

What was clear in Peebels was if you didn't act like a stereotypical gay man then the town was at a loss as to how to treat you. In JB's case, when he did come out he made a whole bunch of the men in town very nervous. He knew some things about them that they didn't want anyone else to know. Embarrassing sex related kind of stuff. What was done behind closed doors. So those people were just as glad when JB left.

Howard, who stayed, after 1969 and Stonewall, finally came out himself. He got by because he was the local newspaper reporter and could have made too many tale's public. He didn't, so he was tolerated. Any other gay men in town tended to keep their lives hidden, away from the public eye.

JB's sister, Sara, had driven over to pick him up in Wichita, which had the closest airport big enough to handle large aircraft. JB was slouched in a plastic chair surrounded by his bags when she walked up wearing jeans, flip-flops, and one of those workout tops artistically torn so one shoulder was bare in a Jennifer Beals-ian/*Flashdance* copy-cat style.

"Well, aren't you quite the little maniac," JB said.

Sara shrugged and held out her arms. "Want to dance?" Then giggled at her joke.

at you," JB answered. "But isn't that look a little out of date?"

"Maybe in New York, but not here."

"Ah, Kansas, always a little late to the party. Back East

we're more into *Benetton* and *Ralph Lauren*." They had fallen into their old roles right from the get go.

As they drove toward Peebels in a tangerine colored taxicab Sara filled him in on what the charges were against Howard.

"It's all very flimsy circumstantial evidence, Older Brother. Even the drug bust was executed under some pretty questionable hearsay."

"I'm going to have to talk to the Police Chief. What do you know about him?"

Sara pondered a moment. "I think he's a good Chief actually. He simply doesn't want any scandal to touch his department. And this murder of one of his cops is already doing that. Rumors are that Vince...that was his name, Vince Barkley...was having sex with a prostitute when he was killed. Or with someone. You know Molly? She's the only whore in town now. She says she didn't do it. If she didn't, then it must have been some other woman. There were lipstick traces around the cop's penis."

"Wait a minute. Did you just say penis?"

"That's what it is, Older Brother."

"But it's a word I hoped you wouldn't throw around like sofa pillows."

"Good God, you need to get home more often. I've been using swear words since I was ten."

Sara was a late child for their mother—there was a seventeen years difference between JB and Sara. Their mother had been as surprised as the rest of the town. Poor mother had supplied at least a week's juicy gossip for everyone when Sara was born. Then she had grown up to be a nice, pretty, responsible young woman. She had even taken over JB's family's transportation company when their father had passed several years before. JB's mother couldn't do it, and Sara had a year of business school behind her by then so she was perfect for the job. Their father had owned the local school bus company, the local cab company—which explained why JB was riding in the front seat of a tangerine colored car with a meter in the space usually reserved for a radio—and had even managed to get the rent-a-truck franchise for not only the town but the entire county. Sara had taken over and ran it better than their father ever had. She was only twenty-four now and had already been written up by the state locals as an exceptional business woman destined to go to the top of her profession.

She dropped JB off at the hotel and they arranged to meet

in a couple of days for dinner.

JB wasn't in his room more than fifteen minutes when there was a knock on the door. He opened it to find Howard's sister standing there. Her arm was up, about ready to knock again.

"Shirley, I was going to call you."

"Can I come in? I wanted to talk to you. About Howard."

"Of course. I just got in. How is Howard?"

She got one of those looks that said there was a lot she had to tell him. He sat on the bed. Shirley stayed standing. Then started pacing.

"He feels like he's being had, JB. Blamed as a scapegoat for a murder he didn't have anything to do with. He thinks its so they can wipe the cop killing off their books. JB, this is rotten to the core. Howard's hoping you can clear him of the whole business." She opened her bag and started rummaging, then pulled out a ten by fourteen manila envelope. She held it out to JB. "This is all of Howard's notes on the story that got him into this mess. From what I understand its about this secret cop club that's here in town. I don't know the details, but the notes should fill you in. Howard told me to give them to you to look over before you see him tomorrow morning."

JB took the envelope. It was heavy. "Wow," he said. "This is a lot, Shirley. I'm not even familiar with all the facts yet. I think I'd better see Howard first before I look at this." He put the envelope in the desk drawer. "You said I'm supposed to see him tomorrow? How do I get that going?" JB looked over at her.

Shirley hadn't aged all that well. She had been the prettiest girl in her class in high school. She had even won Miss Wichita, on her way to being Miss America, but lost at state when she was eighteen. Now, at thirty-eight, she had the same amount of extra pounds on her petite frame. It had settled on her hips, rear, and thighs. That's a problem in small towns; everybody knows your exact age and weight. You can't even cheat by a year or an ounce. She was still attractive in a rounded out way, but wore no make-up, her dark hair in a short cropped 50's duck-tail. She was wearing a pair of shapeless hospital scrubs, a flowered top and blue cotton bottoms, with those clunky white leather work shoes that nurses tend to wear. She was probably on her way to or from work. It wasn't a particularly attractive look for her, but gave her an efficient competent air that probably went over well on the floor at the local hospital where she worked. "First, you'll have to see the Chief," she went on. "He told me to tell you that you need to talk to him first."

"So, I'll make an appointment."

"You don't have to. He said to meet him tomorrow morning, at seven, over at the *Woolworth's* cafeteria."

"I've been ordered to appear, I guess. Who is this guy?"

"You probably know him. He was on the force when we were kids. Chief Rotelli."

"Old Ironpants?" "Ironpants" Rotelli had been a patrol cop who had made JB's life a misery back when he was a teenager. The guy was always trying to catch JB in some trouble or other. JB had acted out some when he was younger. Now Ironpants was the Chief?

Shirley chuckled. "That's the one. But we don't call him that anymore. He's much too important. At least in his own mind. *Woolworth's* is where he has his breakfast every morning."

"Well, breakfast will be on me then. But, this ain't at Tiffany's, that's for sure."

After Shirley left the rest of the day stretched out in front of JB. He could have pulled out the galleys he'd brought with him but he was feeling restless. Being cooped up in an airplane next to a talkative little lady who, after she found out JB was a writer, swore she was the next Barbara Cartland would do that.

The restlessness also made sitting around his hotel room an unattractive proposition. JB got his key, locked the room, and went down to the lobby. Maybe there was something there that would occupy his mind. He was being an optimist.

Beyond the front desk and a tiny newsstand, there were only a couple of chairs sitting next to a round table covered with old newspapers. JB sat in one of the chairs and picked up the local paper. The headline was in 85 point type and said "STAR REPORTER ARRESTED". The story gave JB the facts that both Shirley and his sister had already told him plus a few others he hadn't known.

Such as Howard had been found at the scene of the crime. Vince Barkley, the victim, had been strangled, and the police suspected foul play. It also gave him the location of the crime. Out at Parker Park.

He remembered that Sara had told him that the park had been pretty much abandoned when Mr. Parker died several years before, and was now going back to the wild. What had Howard, and for that matter, the cop been doing out there? He decided he needed to go out to the location and check it out for himself. But he didn't have transportation. He needed wheels.

And his family owned a cab company. Synergy, right?

It took him about fifteen minutes to walk over to the offices of the Peebels Cab Company. When he walked in he was surprised to see Shirley sitting at the reception desk and talking on the phone. JB guessed that she was leaving work when he saw her earlier and she was second jobbing it here at the cab company.

She hung up the phone and said, "We meet again. I help out here every once in a while."

"Really? Is Sara here? I have a favor to ask."

"She's out in the garage. Can I help?"

"Well, I need a car to drive around while I'm here. Think you can get me one?"

"Probably. I don't think Sara would mind one of the partners having a car. But let me check." The proprietorship of the firm had been split between Sara, his mother, and JB when his father passed. As an absentee owner JB didn't have much to do with the workings of the place. That was all Sara's doings.

Shirley left the office and came back a few minutes later with a set of keys. "Sara said you shouldn't do any speeding, and she'd meet you at Triggers tomorrow night for that dinner you promised."

"Tell her it's a date."

He ended up with one of the older model taxi's that had seen better days. It ran, but it chugged and sputtered as JB got used to driving a stickshift again. Painted the same ugly tangerine color that had embarrassed JB for most of his youth, now it didn't seem so bad—it would serve to get him around town at least. The color, still ugly, seemed less offensive considering he was in need of wheels. Beggers. Choosers.

JB took the highway out of town, drove for several miles, and then missed the turnoff for the park. He swung back around, found the turn, and drove over the rutted torn up black-topped road for about a mile in. Until he ran up on the concrete bridge that went to the entrance of the old park itself. He stopped, put the car in parking gear, and got out.

It had become really rustic out here, he thought as he looked around. He checked his watch. It had taken him about twenty-seven minutes to get here, not counting the wrong turn back on the highway. He could see the abandoned entrance to the park across the way. The posts that had held the sign that crossed over the road had rotted and the sign itself now lay catty-corner on the road, its paint peeling, a P and a k the only letters still visible.

It was sad. When JB had been a teenager Parker Park was the place to go on a summer week-end. There was a trout stocked lake that featured a sand beach for sunbathing, and there were rowboats for rent. There was a dance pavilion for record hops, a hamburger stand, and late at night it had been the local lover's lane, the lake ringed with cars holding teenagers exploring the boundaries of petting. Getting to second base was cause for parties and fireworks.

JB went to the edge of the bridge and looked down. There was a strip of yellow police tape strung across the entrance to under the bridge. Was that where the murder took place? That wasn't in the paper. Why was the cop down there?

JB went to the path that led down, taking steps that had been cut into the dirt. He stood by the tree and peered in. It wasn't that wide a bridge, so there was enough light to see clearly. It was dirt under there, mud in many places from left over rain puddles that had stagnated and were growing God knew what kind of diseases. There was a swarm of mosquito's that probably carried malaria hovering over the biggest of the puddles. There was a grouping of crushed cigarettes over on the left. JB didn't know if they were from the crime scene or from the cops that had trampled the hell out of the area. A dirt path, really two wheel ruts in the hard ground with tall grass in between, led down to the underbridge on the other side. It took a gentle curve back up to the road and connected about thirty feet back from where he'd parked his cab. JB slid under the tape and walked to the other side. There wasn't much he could have figured from there, the dirt had been mangled from all the cars that had been around since the killing. A hundred tire tracks had obliterated anything that might have been useful. JB climbed back up to the road and went back to his car. He opened the door and before he got in he bent and scraped the mud from under the bridge off the soles of his shoes. Shouldn't make a mess in a borrowed car, right?

JB, the next morning, met the Chief as requested at the *Woolworth's* lunch counter. You had to go into a special door to get in since the store itself wasn't open yet. JB figured they opened the counter so early only because the Chief wanted his morning meal. Over the past twenty years he had become a medium man. Medium build, medium brown hair, medium height, medium paunch at his belt. It was the uniform that gave him any authority he might have had. It was sharp. Pressed and creased to perfection.

"Well, I never thought I'd see you back here again, Jeremy Bent."

The Chief—Old Ironpants—was only seven or eight years older than JB. He had been, back in the day, a newly discharged military MP who had taken on a job as a small town street cop when JB was a teenager. Ironpants thought he was hot stuff driving around in his patrol car then. He and JB had a few run-ins back in the 50's. There were a few instances of teenage mischief—Halloween pranks, minor shoplifting, nothing serious. But from Ironpant's then inexperienced perspective JB was pegged as a hardcore juvenile offender when he was all of thirteen. In Ironpants's eyes, JB was doomed to a life of crime. Officer Ironpants had also wasted an inordinate amount of time watching JB wherever he went. That made JB's teenage years more difficult and often downright intolerable.

"Chief. I assure you that I am not the boy that left Peebels twenty years ago."

"I should say not. Living up there in New York, writing all those queer mysteries. I've kept my eye on you. You sell a lot of those fag books, do you, Jeremy Bent?"

Good God, could the man still be holding a grudge, after all this time? Could he still be that obsessive over a few candy bars and some *Juicy-Fruit* taken from the five and ten cent store?

"I have my fans," JB offered. "What I wanted to talk to you about, Chief, was about getting permission to see Howard Fellows. He's being held in your jail."

"I know what you want, Bent. But, let me tell you what I want."

"And, what's that, Chief?"

"I want this whole mess to go away, to be honest. I have a very well-run force here in Peebels. I want it to stay that way."

"Chief, I haven't a clue as to what you mean. I'm here to see my oldest friend who's in trouble. When can I do that?"

"You can see him at ten this morning. I made all the arrangements."

"Good, then enjoy your breakfast." JB turned to leave, then turned back. "By the way, Chief..."

The Chief swiveled back on his stool toward JB.

"The alleged murder charge against Howard. Who was the victim again?"

"One of my best officers. A ten year man. Vince Barkley. Found in his car with a rope around his neck. Strangled."

"While having sex I heard? I also heard there were lipstick traces around his...uh...member, which would indicate it was a woman that the victim was with. So, why are you holding Howard?"

"Because, Howard Fellows had a grudge against the guy. They'd had run-ins before. Howard was accusing Barkley of being crooked. He caught Barkley while he was having sex and killed him in the argument that followed."

"Then you arrested the woman too?"

"No. Not at all. She wasn't there."

"Then where was she?"

"Howard must have told her to leave. To protect her from being arrested."

"Has he admitted to that?"

"Well, no. But he will. We're questioning him."

"With rubber hoses and cattle prods?"

"We go strictly by the book here, Bent. Howard was caught at the scene of the crime. He did it."

"I'm not so sure, Chief. There are way to many holes in that theory of yours."

"Holes or not, we're charging Howard Fellows with obstruction and first degree murder in County Court this afternoon."

"Today? And the county attorney went along with it? On such flimsy evidence?"

"We work together on these cases. Howard's only being arraigned this afternoon. We'll get the evidence we need before we go to trial. You wait and see."

"Chief, I'm sorry, but I think you're wrong. Howard couldn't have killed your cop. He's not the type. I would never write him as a killer. As a snoop and a busybody maybe. That's stock and trade for any newspaper reporter. But not a killer."

"Bent, he was found at the scene of the crime. That makes him guilty in my book."

"That makes him at the wrong place at the wrong time, Chief. Not a murderer."

"Bent, I've read about you up in New York solving their cases and writing books about the experience. Well, I'm not so sure that will fly here in Kansas."

"Isn't that what Capote did a few years ago?"

"Yes, and we still haven't lived it down. We can figure this out for ourselves, without your help. Keep your nose clean, Bent."

"I don't know what you mean, Chief. I'm here for..."

"I know, an old friend. Don't get in trouble, Bent. That's all I'm saying."

"Of course, Chief. Say, why don't you call me JB? All my friends do." He left the store.

Getting in to see Howard wasn't the first time JB had been to a jail. Not as a prisoner, mind you, but for visiting purposes and research. Kansas procedures were basically the same as New York's. Gates that opened with keys, doors that were opened by guards. Until you were finally alone in a room waiting for the prisoner.

The room held a table and a couple of chairs with a wire meshed window looking down on it. The table had a large steel eye screwed into its center, and the chairs were stationed one on each side. JB took a seat on the side closest to the door he had come in.

The door on the other side of the room opened and Howard was shuffled in by a guard. He was in a white T-shirt and orange cotton pants that tied at the waist. There was a link chain that went from ankle to ankle and up to a pair of handcuffs at his wrists. He looked as if he hadn't slept very well. Probably not, considering his circumstances. He also looked like he had gained a few pounds since JB had last seen him. Mostly muscle if the arms sticking out from his T-shirt were any indication. It looked like he had started working out. And he was still a handsome devil.

He came over to the table where the guard used his key to take off the cuffs and attach them to the eye screwed into the table. The guard then went outside the room and stationed himself to the side of the partly open door.

JB indicated the cuffs. "A bit melodramatic don't you think?"

Howard turned his head. "Hey, George, he didn't fall for it. You can unlock me now." He grinned and suddenly JB could see the boy that had been his best friend all those years ago Howand was still that kid despite the intervening years. And JB still felt the same love for him he had then and wasn't the least bit surprised to find he still had now. For that's what Howard Fellows would always be to JB—his fist love. The one you never forget and always hold dear.

George came back in, then unlocked and removed both the hand and the leg irons. Then he said, "You owe me fifty, you know? I told you he wouldn't fall for it." He turned to face JB. "How ya doing, kiddo?"

George was a friend of JB's from high school, a part of his crowd, not Howard's. "Great. You and Marge still together?"

"Of course. She still puts up with my bullshit, and I put up with her snoring. I don't think its a fair deal but Marge seems happy." He left the room.

JB looked at Howard. "I was best man at his wedding."

"He didn't tell me that. Hey, I was suckered."

"Not the first time as I recall."

JB's mind went back over the years. At around thirteen and fourteen JB and Howard used to play "Chipmunk" with each other. You know? Searching for nuts. Their wrestling always led to them having sex together. Horny teenagers. But it wasn't until JB left town that Howard had finally admitted he was gay to him. Right as JB was leaving town. Timing wasn't one of Howard's strongpoints.

JB's moving away hadn't done much to keep them close either. The last time the two had talked they only managed about three minutes of stilted conversation, then there was a long silence. JB mentioned that it didn't seem right, that two people who had known each other since they were youngsters didn't have anything to say to each other. Howard agreed. And that was the last time they spoke, oh, in 6 years or so. But JB always thought of Howard with jubilent reminisence. He knew they still cared for each other. Howard was JB's friend, enough said.

"You didn't like my joke? It seemed somehow appropriate. Come on, JB, we used to kid around all the time."

JB put on a stern voice. "When we were teenagers, Howard. Children. We are now mature adults."

"It wasn't all that long ago."

"How old are you? I'll be forty-two on my next birthday."

"And, I'm five and a half months younger. Its always been that way."

"And does that get me any respect? I'm a famous writer now. You're only a picayune small town news jockey. Remember that, please."

"Now wait a second..."

"Who's pulling your chain, you idiot." JB grinned. "We're both grown-up now. We might only have some old history to keep us together though. Like the long married couple who wouldn't let go of each other's hands."

"Huh?"

"If they did they'd kill each other. Now what's the story on all this? What are you doing here?"

"You should audition for *Star Search,* JB. You're sure to win the worst comic category?"

Howard and JB had bickered back and forth the same way as kids. It had been considered fun to put each other down back then. JB now did the same busting chops thing with his friend, Len Matthews, back in New York. The remarks were often cutting, and always expressed with infinate affection, even if any bystander wouldn't believe it if he heard it. It was a clue to their relationship that Howard and JB so quickly fell back into it, a testament to their friendship even when they weren't in touch. It may have looked like they didn't care, but they did care enough to come to each other's aid when needed. JB knew that now was one of those times.

"Howard?"

"Okay, first I was arrested for being involved in a drug ring here in town. It's a lie, of course. I've never messed with drugs in any way. Ever. I was aware of the drug trafficking going on in town , of course. I was after a story from one of the gang members. Guy named Randy. He's in here now too, as a matter of fact."

"I know you weren't involved with drugs, Howard. You always thought taking aspirin was a sign of weakness."

"Right. The Chief couldn't make that accusation stick so now I'm going to be charged with the murder of Vince Barkley. The meanest, but I have to say the hunkiest cop on the force. You should have seen him, JB. He was gorgeous. Muscles out to there. He was the reason I started going to the gym. To watch the guy. I swear he was the prettiest man this side of Hyde Lake. But, I didn't kill him. Having a crush on him and killing him are two different things."

"I'm glad you know the difference. But it doesn't explain why they think you killed him."

"Oh, well, we did have a history."

"And that was?"

"I was blackmailing him."

JB stared at Howard for a long moment, then finally said, "And what was that about?"

"I promised him that if he gave me all the dope on this underground gay cop club I found out about here in town, then I wouldn't expose him as one of the town's leading faggots."

"Howard? I hate that word. And you know it."

"Oh. Okay, pansy."

"I don't know if that's any better, but I'll accept it. So, you were going to out him, is that it?" It was a term just then coming into use in New York. Outing was the publishing of men's and women's names who were closeted, known to be gay, but hidden, and perceived as hurting the gay movement from achieving its goals. It was very controversial.

"I was going to use it against him so I could write an exposé on small town gay life. Its all underground here, JB. So, yeah, I was going to out him. Is that what you big city boys call it? Here nobody talks about it? The article would have got me an award. It would have got me to Wichita. On the paper over there."

"Howard you're over forty years old, and you've been on the local paper here since high school. You're here in Peebels like solid rock. Get used to it."

"Hey, I'm pretty well known over in Wichita. I only need enough money to make the move. And I've finally got that covered. So, when Mother goes, I'm gone. You know I stay here only because of Mother."

Howard's mother, Vivian, was a real piece of work. She was always difficult. Watching over Howard like he was precious cargo. Cloying and overbearing. After Howard's dad died of cancer, Vivian took to her bed. A heart problem she claimed. Some said she was faking it to get sympathy. Whatever, she was bedridden much of the time. Howard and Shirley had become responsible for caring for her. So the three of them rattled around in that old Victorian they called home. Most of its eighteen rooms were closed off as it cost a fortune to heat and with Vivian an invalid they didn't use most of the place anyway. Vivian was a demanding old bird. She'd also become evil minded and cruel as the years passed. And now she refused to die. Here she was in her seventies, and it looked like she was one of those who would go on until a hundred.

"But, Howard, do you have to stay in jail? What about bail?"

"I haven't been arraigned yet. Bails not been set. This afternoon" He turned to the door. "Right, George?"

George spoke through the partly open door. "At three."

"Until then, I'm part of the general population of the Peebels City Jail. Me and three other guys. And one of them is in the drunk tank. I think I'll read a book. They have a pretty good library for a one horse hoosegow. I might even read one of your little efforts."

"Three? With trial time factored in you won't be out until tomorrow morning. I'll pick you up. I have one of the company taxi's."

"Then its a date." Howard leaned back and reached into his pant's pocket. He pulled out his fist and held it out to JB. "Keep this for me, will you? I'll get it back when we see each other tomorrow."

"Okay. What is it?" Howard's fist opened and a gold key dropped into JB's hand.

"The key to the story that'll get me out of Peebels. Haven't you been listening?"

"As I said, in your dreams." JB put the key in his pocket. "Now, so I can start figuring how to get these charges against you dropped, tell me everything you know about this. Including that gay cop club you mentioned."

After their visit JB spent the rest of the day in his room. He had intended to get to work on his galleys, but first he pulled out the envelope of Howard's notes Shirley had left with him. And that's exactly what they were. Pieces of paper, napkins, *Post-Its* with jottings in Howard's unreadable scribble on them. Some had dates with a couple of names, some had whole paragraphs with sentences crossed out and revised. As a writer himself JB understood what went into making up a story, so the jumble of notes wasn't all that difficult for him to understand. He had a file of exactly the same thing back in New York. JB was well aware that ideas and information could come at you at any time and any scarp of paper would do to get the idea down. Besides, JB was a puzzle freak and figuring out Howards thinking processes was amusement for him.

He started reading each of the scraps and was getting the string of Howard's thoughts when he came upon a piece of lined notebook paper that had almost a whole story written out on it. Was Howard trying his hand at fiction? JB leaned back on the bed and read.

The story concerned two women in a small town. Write about what you know was always good advice. One of the women was a nurse, the other a business owner. They were named Trish and Terry. They had been friends for many years and had become close. And they were having a lesbian affair.

Wait a second? Trish and Terry? Not a giant leap from that to Sara and Shirley?

Was Howard writing about their sisters? Was Sara a lesbian? Was Shirley? Was it possible? Could his sister be gay? My God, its hereditary. It runs in the family? Okay, this was too much to swallow in one spoonful.

JB put the rest of the notes back in their envelope and then put the envelope back in the desk drawer. Then he re-read Howard's story. The facts hadn't changed. It intimated in clear news like storytelling that there were two women in Peebels having a lesbian affair. And other facts pointed straight, if you'll pardon the expression, at their sisters. It left JB wondering what he should do. Should he confront Sara? Or hint around until she confessed? Wait a minute, maybe it *was* simply a piece of fiction on Howard's part. He would have to wait until the next morning to find out. When he met Howard at the police station.

JB decided to work on the galleys he had brought with

him to correct. Galleys were the first printing off the presses of a new book. His publisher sent him pages that on that particular book were two pages wide and three pages long printed both front and back. When folded they became the leaves of JB's latest novel. There were twelve pages on a single sheet, and they were twenty-seven sheets thick. That would make a three hundred and thirty-seven page book.

JB got the galleys from his briefcase and sat them down on the desk. He then pulled out the original manuscript and put it side by side with the galleys. That way he could compare one against the other, page by page. He got a red pen, a copy of his list of printers marks, and began to read.

He got involved in marking out incorrect commas, putting back missing capital letters, and changing proper nouns. But his mind would keep going back to the question. Was Sara gay? He knew that since he didn't live in town any more that they weren't as close as they could have been. He hadn't been around when Sara was growing up so they hadn't formed as close a bond as many brothers and sisters. But JB spoke with Sara and his Mother weekly. Sara could have told him at anytime. Why would she keep this a secret? Well, he figured, she does live in Peebels. It's a small town that thrives on gossip and innuendo about any and all of its citizens. But that wasn't an excuse to keep it from him. Sara knew he wouldn't have condemned her, didn't she? How could he? He'd been rowing the same boat before he left town. So why would she not tell him?

Before he was aware time had passed and it was seven o'clock at night. That had got him through a whole thirty pages of a more than three hundred page manuscript. This was going way too slow. The typesetter had to have been reading some other writers book while he was typing JB's. The problem was he wasn't sure he could get the project done in time.

Len was tidily ensconced in a hotel in San Francisco because he had been hired to play Captain Hook, every character actors dream part, in a road show company of *Wendy and Hook*, a new play that continued the adventures of the J.M. Barrie characters from *Peter Pan*. It was a children's musical and story, with enough flash and whimsy to appeal to adults as well. The company was taking it across country as a try-out run hopefully headed for New York.

The company had already played LA for five weeks previously and had spent three of a four week engagement in San Francisco so far. Len loved San Francisco, not only because it was the gayest city in the entire world—although Amsterdam ran it a close second—but it was a perfectly beautiful place to be. The Twin Peaks views with the ocean beyond, Golden Gate Park, Coit Tower. Lovely. And the weather was mild and wonderful. Where summer in New York was oppressive and muggy—a person could grow mushrooms in their armpits there—in San Francisco the bay breezes kept it temperate and cool. And it was a terrific theatre town. San Franciscans loved their plays, and were attentive and enthusiastic audiences.

The production had started rehearsals back in New York about three months before, and was on its second engagement on the West Coast, planning to head across country so they could be in New York for the holiday season. There was talk of a Broadway run, but that depended on how the show went over while out here in the hinterlands.

A lot depended on the woman playing Wendy. She wasn't the sugary sweet girl the producers had written for the show. Not at all. She was a show-business savey one-hit pop singer now with legit show business aspirations. She made Ethel Merman look like *The Sweetheart of Sigma Chi*, although she did know how to play against type and do cute. Len wasn't so sure that one top 40 hit in the early eighties would be enough to get audiences in to see her. But, like all actors, Len also knew that work was work—you grabbed it where you could. Besides the show credit, as the irresistible Captain Hook, would look very good on his resume, even if the sweetness of the show's plot was enough to make grown men gag. The show was quickly becoming a basis for jokes throughout the theatrical community. The book was that the pirate's under Hook's command had gone on strike unless they were told bedtime stories the same as Pan's Lost Boys. So, what else would they do? Hook, and his second mate, Sneed, kidnap Wendy to do it. Hopefully, riotous situations ensued, including Hook romantically involved with a wacky Countess, all accompanied by charming songs and dancing Indian maids, swimming mermaids and comic pirates.

Len was really quite pleased to be working in what could easily become one of the biggest shows in New York. There were few shows aimmed at children on Broadway, and if produced and presented at the right time, meaning Christmas, this one could have every vacationing kid in the tri-county area at their theatre. Both in San Francisco and LA it had been marginally well received. Reviews from the critics were quietly enthusiastic—personal reviews for Len had been quite good, less so for the pop-star. The producers were hoping she would grow stronger in the role as she performed across the country. That meant the show was at least headed for Denver next week. That was if there weren't any more of these unexplained accidents to keep the show from moving on.

The morning after Wendy's fall, Len found a notice shoved under his hotel room door for a cast call at the theatre at noon.

He tried calling JB again, got no answer, so went down to the lobby planning to head for the hotel restaurant for an early lunch. As he went past the bar he spotted the woman who was playing The Countess, his love interest in the play, wrapped in a mink coat and settled in a booth. There was a full to the brim cocktail glass in front of her.

Len went over to her table. "Countess?" he said.

The cast on the show had been calling everyone by their character names since New York. It started when the director first did it. He had admitted he was terrible with names and calling everyone by the name of their parts was easier than trying to remember their real monikers. The cast members had then picked it up from him. That was helped along when they'd named the director The Croc. As a cost-cutting device, and since he was an ex-dancer, he was playing the part of the crocodile in the show. Unusual for a director, but it was a small part with no lines and it meant he could travel with the show and make any changes needed as they wended their way toward New York.

The woman playing the Countess was a well-known and popular second leading lady, the star's best friend on a now defunct TV series. She was a good steady actress and a hoot to be around. She was what was kindly called a broad by those who knew her, and with the heavy layer of wacky she placed on top of her part she was perfect as Len's foil in the play. She also was rumored to have a slight drinking problem. Len knew all about that particular slippery slope from his own experience.

"Isn't it a bit early for that?" Len indicated the glass on the table.

"My Captain," she said. "I'm just waiting for lunch. As a chaser to my Sex On The Beach..." She held up her glass. "Anyway, it must be afternoon in New York." She pushed up the sleeve of her coat. "Where's my watch? I never can keep track of time." She looked up at Len. "And it's even later in Paris, I'll bet." She hooted. "That's good enough for me. You want to join me?"

"For lunch? Sure. But I'll skip the libation."

"Your loss." Referring to the show, she said, "Won't help you get your sea legs though. That dance of yours could use some loosening up." Len had a dance as Hook that, with the help of Tinkerbell's magic powder, had him literially dancing on the ceiling. Done with slip-on shoe clamps and a ball-bearing track it simulated dance turns on a rail that slid along the roof beam of the cabin set.

"I'm still not used to the clamps that hold me to the track." Len defended himself. "And I haven't got the turns right yet." Len slid into the banquette. "Hook appearing in a body cast wouldn't be that funny. We've already got one cast member in one."

The Countess put on a pained expression. "That was a bit insensitive, My Captain. A reminder of last nights accident. Poor Wendy. Is she all right?"

"Did you get the notice for the noon call?" She nodded. "I have a feeling it's to rehearse her understudy. I can't see our original girl going on any time soon. That shoulder was very painful for her."

"Who's her replacement?'

"The girl who's currently playing Princess Tom-Tom."

"But, she's only a kid."

"She's seventeen and playing younger, Countess. I guess we'll have to start calling her New Wendy from now on. Kind of catchy, huh? New Wendy. But I think it'll be interesting having a girl the right age playing the part of Wendy Darling. Instead of our almost twenty-five something teen idol. Don't you think?"

It's a fact of life in the theatre that professional child actors are usually older than the age of their parts. That's true throughout the business, even on TV. That's why you get programs with high school boys who have five o'clock shadows instead of down and girls with 38C's instead of *Little Angel's*. An older child actor is easier for the staff and crew to work with. On this show, for instance, it meant fewer teenagers needing daily schooling, which was another cost saving device, since the tutor charged by the number of children she handled. Also, older children's attention spans were better; they stayed more focused on the job at hand. The original Wendy, who had sprained her shoulder the night before, was twenty-five and made-up every night to look younger. Even the boy who played Sneed, who was supposed to be seventeen or eighteen—since the producers had written a sub-plot of a romance between Sneed and Wendy—was a well trained professional juvenile who had turned twenty-one the year before. He only still looked boyish. The child playing the youngest Indian maid, who was supposed to be eight, was really twelve. She was just short.

"I suppose New Wendy can be made-up to look older than she's been looking."

"Exactly. By the way, you know that wasn't an accident."

"What wasn't?"

"Last night. I had a chance to check out the plank. It had been sawed so it would break."

"You're joking? Aren't you?"

"Unfortunately, no. And now I'm thinking that the other accidents we've had were deliberate too. Someone is trying to sabotage our show."

"But whatever for? I know its on the sugary side, but that's no reason to stoop to subversion."

"Humm, now that sounds like something Oscar Wilde should have written..."

Hook and Wendy had, even as far back as New York and the rehearsals, several accidents happen to it already. Mostly little annoyances. Missing props, costumes damaged, sets rearranged, that kind of thing. But this latest incident was out and out malevolent. And since Wendy was injured it made a big difference to the show.

The new girl, New Wendy, was a competent actress to be sure, but seemed to Len very young even for seventeen. If someone can play thirteen convincingly when their older it might be a reflection on that person's real maturity level. Many child actors, although effective, have little real training. They don't know why or how they create the effect they do.Their technique is based on pure personality. Sweet and perky, as New Wendy certainly was, could only carry a girl so far. Somewhere along the line she had to bring talent with her. Len wasn't so sure New Wendy had what it took.

Countess said, "The girl only has the one solo as a feature. The rest is larger group stuff. I suppose we can work around her."

"Maybe," Len agreed. "But, I think I'll reserve judgement until she plays tonight. Although I hope the girl will surprise us. That's what her mother keeps assuring us of. We'll find out, I guess."

The girl's mother was also a member of the company, working both as a chaperone for the younger kids, and playing a cantina whore in the pirate's lair in the ensemble. Again, it's a fact that all plays use people in multiple capacities. The children's tutor, just graduated from college with her degree, was also playing a mermaid. One of the pirate crew handled the light that represented Tinkerbell in the play.

"Well. She would, wouldn't she?" Countess slapped the table lightly. "I've never met a pushier stage mother than that woman. Even mine wasn't that bad, and mine made Cinderella's stepmother look like *Mrs. Miniver.*"

"She does seem to have tunnel vision when it comes to her daughter. She's been trying to get that kid into Wendy's part since New York. Hey, do you think she might be the saboteur? So her daughter could play?"

"No, she couldn't have gone that far. Could she? It's just a part in a play."

"Wasn't there a mother who put a hit on another cheerleader so her daughter could be head of the squad? In Texas, I think?"

"Captain, you have to go to The Croc with this."

"I don't think the director will much care. He only wants people in the parts that can play. And to be honest, this is all guesswork on my part so far. I have no proof that it's really happening."

"Then you need to look into it. Find out who this is. I'll not go all the way across country with a dangerous maniac in the show."

"I could have some quiet talks with some of the cast. See what I can get out of them. See if they think it could be sabotage. Is that a good idea?"

The Countess nodded.

Notes From Home

The next morning JB was in his cab parked out in front of the jailhouse waiting for Howard. A deputy leaned into the window and told him the Chief wanted to see him.

He climbed out and followed the guy into the building. They went down a dingy corridor and stopped in front of the Chief's office door. The deputy knocked. The Chief yelled, "Come." The deputy opened the door and waved JB in.

The Chief was sitting behind his desk. As JB walked across the room, he stood from a massive executive black leather chair that literally dominated the room. It was huge, even more impressive than the desk it sat behind. He pointed. "Have a seat, JB. I have something to tell you."

That's one of the things JB always appreciated about people in Kansas. Straight to the point. No niceties. No beating of bushes.

"What's happened to Howard?" JB asked.

"Who said anything about Howard?"

"Chief, the only reason I'm in Peebels to begin with is Howard. Unless it concerned Howard I'd have no business knowing anything about whatever you want to tell me."

"Aren't you the star detective."

"What about Howard?"

"Uh, he died last night." Straight to the point, right?

"What? How?" JB was flabbergasted. Howard dead? "Does his sister know?"

The Chief sat and leaned back in his chair. The back of it rose at least eight or nine inches above his head. With all the tufts and brass nailheads surrounding his head it made him look like he was laid out in a coffin. The curved wings on the sides of the chair added to the funereal illusion. Missing was the scythe and black hood needed for the information he was passing on. "Howard was found this morning hanging in the library. He'd used a sheet as a noose. Was he morose, or depressed, or anything like that, when you talked to him yesterday?"

"No, sir. He was anxious to get out of here. Who could blame him for that? Are you sure it was suicide?"

"What else could it be? They opened his cell when he didn't respond to roll call this morning. He wasn't there. They instigated a search and found him in the library. He was hanging from the water pipes that run along the ceiling."

"It's so out of character for him. I would never have written Howard like that. He was looking forward to going to Wichita. There was no reason for him to kill himself."

"He was facing charges for killing Vince Barkley. That might have got to him."

"Charges that he knew were bogus, Chief. Howard thought he was set up by your cop for trying to blackmail him into telling about a cop club within this force. He was supposed to meet Barkley that night to get the information. When he got there he found Vince dead in the passenger seat of his car. Then another of your cops drove up. Convenient, what? A murderer caught supposedly still at the scene of the crime. Then you showed up and arrested Howard. Why were you there, Chief?"

"My man found him with Vince and called it in."

"How long before you got to the scene?"

"I got out to the bridge about a half hour after the call."

"That's an old road, Chief. No one goes out there unless they want to be alone. Why was your man out there?"

"He'd tried to call Barkley on his radio and didn't get a response. They were friends. Terry Rickman got worried when his friend didn't call back. He'd found a note from Barkley on his locker telling him that if he wasn't back at the station that night that he would be out there. He was planning on meeting someone, and he wasn't sure what would happen. That give's me Howard's reason for the murder."

"It also gives you from when Barkley went on shift and when your cop found him for someone else to have killed him. When did Barkley start his shift?"

"At nine that night."

"Then he'd just begun work for the night." The Chief nodded. "Give him a half hour to drive out to the bridge. That puts it at nine-thirty or round about. So, it was from nine-thirty until...what was his name? Rickman?"

"That's right."

"Rickman found the dead man. When was that Chief?"

"He made the call at eleven-ten."

"That's two hours, Chief. There could have been a convention of Shriner's out there. Hell, they could have put up their tents, held their circus, and packed back up in that amount of time. Someone else could have murdered Barkley easy. Is that all the evidence you had on Howard? Because Howard told me he had an alibi for the time before he arrived at the scene. That was a few minutes before eleven."

"He was found at the scene of the crime. What more did I need."

"What about the woman? The one Barkley was having sex with. Your cop was found with his pants down. Literally. How did he die? I don't remember."

"Strangulation. There was a rope tied around his neck, and it was made to look like a suicide. He had the other end in his own hands. Though why anyone would try hanging that way is crazy. That's why we suspected murder in the first place. No one would hang themselves that way."

"What way?"

"The rope went over the back of the seat, and around to his hands. He would have had to pull on the rope until he choked? What's wrong with the tree right beside the bridge? That's what I want to know?"

"I think I've heard about this. He wasn't trying to hang himself, Chief. It's a breathing game people play who are into kinky sex. It involves cutting off your breath. A bit of suffocation can make the end come on stronger. Intensify the climax, so they say."

"I knew it," the Chief said. "I knew you'd bring that queer, perverse stuff into this. You homos always gotta go for the dirty stuff. Well, we don't think like that here in Kansas. But, since you live all the way up in New York you've probably been corrupted. I should have expected it."

"Chief, trust me, sex games are not confined to New York City. They are more or less universally known, and played. I'll bet you've even done it." The Chief shook his head vigorously. "Really? When was the last time you and your lady pretended that you were a repairman and she was an unsuspecting housewife? Or the mailman and the lonely hausfrau. That's game playing, Chief. Basically, if you have an imagination you'll play some sort of sex games. Admittedly, some people have more vivid imaginations than others. If it doesn't hurt anyone else, what's the harm?"

"Not on my force it doesn't."

"I think you may be wrong. Before I finished my visit with Howard he told me everything he knew. He said he was on the trail of a so-called gay cop club right here in Peebels. How do you know that the woman Barkley was with wasn't a man?"

"A man? Are you saying Vince Barkley was queer? I don't believe it."

"Why not. Men have been known to get together."

"Not in Peebels."

"Everywhere, Chief. We are everywhere you know. There's no reason that your officer and someone from this gay cop group Howard told me about couldn't have got together out there under that bridge for some fun. Then it went bad. That man..." The Chief sat forward, meaning to protest. "...or some woman, if you insist, was your killer. That's who you need to find. And, I think to prove that Howard didn't kill Barkley I need to find out who's in this cop group. You said that another cop found the dead man. What was his name again?"

"Rickman. Terry Rickman."

"And you said he was a friend of the victim. I wonder just how close they were? Where can I find him, Chief?"

"He's off-duty right now. Probably over at Goldy's"

"Goldy's?"

"It's a bar that my officers hang out at. After work. I'll tell you where it is."

"Thanks."

Goldy's was right around the corner from the station. Location, location, location. It hadn't always been called Goldy's.

When JB was a kid it was called the AcesHi. His Dad used to go there to play darts. And to get away from his Mother. Other than the name change it still looked the same on the outside. A brick front. A door with a blacked out glass and a painted martini glass with an olive. Inside was a different matter.

JB stepped in and was surprised by a raucous voice saying, "Oh look, fresh meat. And cute too." The rest of the bar turned to look at him. JB knew immediately what he'd stepped into.

Any bar on Christopher Street in New York would have been proud of this place. There was even a big pink triangle painted on the back mirror. JB had stumbled into a gay bar. Except it wasn't. The place was filled with what appeared to the naked eye to be very straight men. Cops in uniform, mostly. With one or two business-suited types mixed in. Streaks of smoke hung over the bar as if waves roiling on an angry ocean. There was a jukebox on the back wall. And a pool table over to the left. A TV was over at the far end of the bar playing a rerun of *I Love Lucy*. There were about seven or eight men in the place.

JB walked up to the bar and the queen serving behind ambled over. "What can I do ya, ducks?"

"Hi. I'm looking for Terry Rickman. Is he here?"

"I'll cost you a drink for the information. What'll ya have?"

"Oh, sure. A beer. In a bottle."

"Ah, a he-man. I got *Schlitz*, or *Pasbt Blue Ribbon*."

"The first."

Goldy turned and went back to the beer chest. He was back in a few seconds with a bottle. He sat it down in front of JB. "Rickman is over there. Playing pool. Say, you're Jeremy Bent. The writer. Aren't you?"

"Yeah."

"Hey, I've read your stuff. The drink is on me. You from here?"

"Yeah. I grew up here."

"And now you're in my place. Who'd a thunk? A famous New York writer here in my place. How neat is that?"

"No, the pleasure's mine. To find another out gay man here in Peebels, and a fan too. That's great. When I got here I half expected a group of grumbling men with torches and a noose to meet me. How do you survive?"

"Here? I'm the town character, dearie. And they love me for it. They think I'm a camp. As if anyone in this burg would recognize camp if it smacked them in the puss. But I supply some shock value in this hellhole."

"So you play at being outrageous?" Times had certainly changed in town. In JB's day this guy would have been put on the first bus to another city, if not stung up to a nearby tree.

"I'm surprised you haven't been run over by a truck. Tolerance was never one of Peebels' strong suits. Wouldn't it be safer if you moved?"

"Can't. All my money's invested in this place. I won't get it back if I move. So here I sit." He stretched out his arms and raised a knee. "A great big queen in a tiny homophobic hole."

"You are very brave, my friend. Now, where did you say Terry Rickman was?"

"He's over there playing pool. But you don't want to mess with him. He's not the most friendly sort. None of those Poker Guys are." This was being said by a man who was sitting at the corner of the bar. JB turned to look at him.

He recognized him immediately. It was Eddie. Eddie Falco. Howard, JB, and Eddie had been acquaintances way back in ninth grade. Later Eddie was the one who got Howard to stop hanging around with JB. That was a few years down the line, when they had all started high-school. Eddie had figured out JB was gay. Not so hard really. JB wasn't exactly Mr. He-man Hercules after all. Lousy at sports. Interested in the arts. He stuck out. Eddie didn't think it looked cool for voted-most-popular Howard to be seen with queer little Jeremy Bent.

"Hello, Eddie."

"JB."

He hadn't changed that much in twenty years. He still lookd like Howdy Doody. But mature. As if the puppet had grown up and gone to business. He still had the same ginger hair, freckled cheeks, and toothy grin. He was wearing a *Brooks Brothers* suit with a good cut. Tailored. Probably altered from the rack. And a rep tie. Conservative. Standard business wear, if you were an uptight travel agent. JB knew that was what Eddie was doing now. JB's mother and sister kept him appraised of what was going on in the lives of the people he used to know in town. Eddie was the owner of the town's only travel agency. His place was on Main Street. Office in front, living quarters in back where he lived alone. Another charming facet of small town life; everybody knows way to much of your business.

Eddie held up his drink. "Let me get you one of these, JB. I heard about Howard this morning. I'm really sorry he's dead. We'll drink to him."

"Eddie, I already have one of those." JB held up his beer.

"And you never wanted Howard to have anything to do with me, so why would I have a drink dedicated to him with you?"

He faced JB on his stool. "Come on, man. That was years ago. Way in the past. Why not let old grudges go?" He started to cross one leg over the other, then thought about it before he finished the action. He pulled the leg back up so that his ankle rested on his knee. This was a common enough phenomenon among straight men. They get around a known gay man and suddenly they up the manly quotient by about sixty-seven degrees. Voices got deeper, stances take on a John Wayne swagger, gestures get sharper and more aggressive. God forbid anyone should think they might have even one tiny queer bone in their entire bodies. As if JB cared?

"Hey, I can help you meet with Rickman. I know him pretty well," Eddie added.

He went on to tell JB that he and Terry, and even the now dead Vince, had done stuff together. They'd been fishing, attended a couple of truck rallies, and shot weapons out at the range. Eddie was even one of the few that had been invited to the Poker Guys poker night. Whatever that was? Again JB saw it as masculine posing. Eddie could have simply said they were friends. It wasn't like JB suspected them of crocheting doilies, or attending the musical theatre together.

"So what did Howard have to do with any of that?" JB asked. He had to admit Eddie was right about one thing. He did need to let go of his resentment toward the man. Ancient grudges would get in the way of him finding out what was going on there in Peebels. Like that Poker Guys thing. What was that all about? Was that the club Howard was talking about? Was it something shady and clandestine? A sinister neo-Nazi anti-gay cabal planning to overthrow liberation movements everywhere? Maybe JB could get some information that could clear Howard by getting himself invited to that poker game. Whatever was going on here was what got Howard killed. Eddie was offering to help JB find out what that was. Why not let him do it? Anything that would grease the wheels and get him inside where people would talk to him.

"All right, Eddie. But forget the drink. An introduction will do fine. But, first, who is he? Tell me about your friend."

"Oh. Okay. Well, Terry Rickman. He's a real piece of work. Meanest bastard in the whole damn town now that Vince is gone. He makes Arnold Schwarzenegger look like a pansy. And he hates faggots. So, you need to butch it up when I take you over there." Then he shrugged. "But, I guess it don't matter. Everybody in Peebels knows that you're a great big fruit." Small towns—as JB had said before, everyone knows your business.

"So, that means I can be myself? Great. And I promise I won't hit him with my purse."

Eddie weakly smiled at JB. As if he wasn't sure he was joking. "What you want to do is get him to play a game of pool with you, JB. He thinks he's the champ in these parts."

"You mean he's seen *The Hustler* one too many times?"

"He's beat most everybody around here."

Goldy piped up. "I'm not so sure that isn't because everybody's afraid of him. They let him win because he's a sore loser."

"Could be," Eddie replied. "But, that's still what you should offer. You can be someone new for him to beat at pool."

Along with their plaid wool *L.L.Bean* shirts, lumberjack boots, and mustaches, one of the requirements to hang out at JB's local Manhattan gay bar was to play a decent game of pool. He'd spent many an hour with his hands around a pool cue. And not because he was playing Professor Harold Hill in a road company of *The Music Man*. In New York he'd played many a game against pro's and gifted amateurs. Hell, he'd even managed to beat some of them. "Good idea. I'll challenge him," JB said.

"He plays for money. You have cash on you?"

"A little."

"Good. Come on. I'll take you over."

It seemed patently obvious to JB that he had to win this cop Rickman's respect very quickly or he might be the next beaten to a pulp, dragged behind a Ford pickup, gay guy in the Peebels homophobic history books. Or, JB could play it like Casper Milktoast and let Rickman win the game. Let's see? Respect if he won, being treated as a shlub if he let Rickman win. Some choice?

Eddie went up to the table while JB stood back and waited. He said something low to Rickman, who stood up from his shot and looked over at JB. Eddie then waved his hand for JB to come over.

Rickman held out his hand as Eddie said, "This guy thinks he can beat you, Terry. You should give him a chance." Rickman took JB's hand and shook it, hard, so that JB winced at the grip the man used.

"Sure, I'll play him. But only if I get something out of it. What'll you give me, fella?"

JB took his hand back. "How about a beer. I'll get you a fresh one."

"Sure. That'll do."

JB indicated to Goldy to bring over two. "I was thinking maybe we could lay a side bet too. Does twenty do it for you?"

"Now you're talking. But I gotta warn you. I always win."

"I'll take my chances."

JB beat the pants off the guy. Which wouldn't have been awful by the way. Rickman was quite good-looking in a high school jock gone over the hill kind of way.

Rickman broke, and caused a flurry of rolling balls that ended with nothing going in. But it did set up the table for JB. He had a run of nine balls. It was remarkable. He couldn't miss. Ball after ball. At the end of the run JB missed a simple straight shot into the pocket, with the ball bouncing off the bumper. Then Rickman was sure he had a bank shot in the bag. He missed. But his miss meant the table was open for JB to finish off the game.

Rickman took getting beaten like, as they say, a man. It didn't look like he was going to beat up on JB anyway. Still JB cringed a little when Rickman threw his arm over his shoulder. He was expecting to be punched. Instead Rickman congratulated him and pulled him close. Then he hauled JB over to the bar so he could buy him a drink. And his arm stayed over JB's back. What the hell? JB started getting uncomfortable. When Rickman's hand went down and squeezed his bicep JB moved away.

"Thanks, Mr. Rickman."

That's when JB saw it. It was the old eye thing. It's something gay men do to each other. Straight guys do it too, but their eyes stop higher up. In gay life the men's eye travels down a new person's body, checking it out, with an obligatory linger at the old twig and berries. Straight's usually stop chest high. Most disconcerting for both sexes was when the eyes didn't come back up. Rickman, surprisingly, did the gay eye thing. He not only lingered on JB's bunch, but he licked his lips. Well, that's interesting, JB thought, not what he would have expected at all, but interesting. Maybe he could take advantage of it? It only took a few minutes for JB to bring up and be invited to the Poker Guys game the next night. He was going to be a fill infor the newly open spot at the table. They were looking for a new guy to sit in Vince's old spot.

"Well, thanks for the invitation, but I won't be staying in town. I'm only visiting. Could I make it just for the one night?"

"No problem," Rickman said. "You can be my special guest. We're allowed to bring a guest to the game any week we want. You'll be my poke for the night." And he leered. JB couldn't believe it. The guy was propositioning him. Right there in public.

"I beg your pardon?"

"Oh, that's what we call guests. Pokes. The club is called the Poker Guys. So you're my poke for tomorrow night's game. Say, what's your name anyway, fella?"

"It's JB. Jeremy Bent."

Rickman got some look on his face. Some shock, some disappointment, some offense.

"Not that faggot writer that grew up here?"

"Well, I did grow up here. But I'm not a bundle of sticks, I'm only gay. Why? Are homosexual's not allowed to play card games in this city?"

"I forgot about you being in town." There was that know all your business thing again. Rickman stood tall and straightened his uniform. "As a matter of fact, faggots aren't all that welcome here. They're usually run out of town."

"Except for me, Rickman," And Goldy did a batting eye, pouting lip routine at him that could make any self-respecting gay man retch. "I get to stay, don't I, sweetheart?" He set down two bottles of beer. JB was dumfounded. If this is what the man had to do to get along there in Peebles JB wasn't so sure he shouldn't take the loss on his bar and get the hell out of town. Humiliation wasn't a positive way of life for anyone. Rickman looked at Goldy with undisguised contempt as he curtsied. "Yeah, Goldy, you stay. But not because I want you to. Because this place would close, and we wouldn't have our hangout if you did leave. But I can only stand one freak here in town at a time. The rest better keep out of my way."

"Or, what?" JB said. "You'll come after them with a rope and strangle them? Isn't that how your friend Vince died? What happened? Did you find out he was queer and try to make him leave town?"

"What the hell are you talking about? Vince wasn't no fag."

"Then Howard couldn't have killed him. Since Vince was having sex when he was killed, and he wasn't gay, then Howard wasn't the one who was in flagrante delicto, delightful, and de-lovely with him."

"Hey, he was found at the scene. How could he not be the prime suspect?"

"So were you out there. Why?"

"I found a note from Vince. It told me where he was."

"How do you know the killer didn't plant the note? So you would be sure to find Howard at the place where the crime had occurred. That way whoever killed the cop threw the blame to somebody else and away from him. Or her. When did you find the note?"

"When I took my break at the station. At ten-thirty. It was taped to the front of my locker."

"And you hadn't been back to your locker since you came on duty. When was that?"

"I started late. At twenty after nine."

"Wait. Vince was out at the bridge by nine-thirty. He would have left you your note before he went on his shift. That was at nine according to the Chief. You would have found the note when you got there late to start your shift. But you didn't find it until you took your break after ten? That proves Barkley didn't leave any note for you."

"Hey, that's pretty good. You figured that out right here? And you made it look easy."

"That looked easy? I'll have you know it takes the same kind of analytical mind that Sherlock Holmes would have had. He was gay by the way. He and Dr. Watson were very happy together. Mrs. Hudson was their hag."

Goldy said, "And Professor Moriarty was into S&M? So, who did kill Vince? If Howard Fellows didn't do it, who did?"

"That's what I intend to find out. So, Rickman, does this mean I won't be playing poker with your little group? Is my being gay a problem for you?"

He hemmed and hawed a little thinking about it. Then JB would have sworn Rickman kicked at an imaginary clump of dirt, as he said, "Naw, your okay. You ain't too faggy at that. And, shit, I like you. You don't take no guff. We'll let you play. The other guys won't argue with me about it. You're my poke, not theirs." His arm went back around JB's shoulder. As JB was being dragged back to the pool table, Goldy indicated that he should talk to him again before he left the place.

JB played another couple of games with Rickman, but didn't learn anything more. Except that the man was a braggart. And a lousy pool player.

Also, there was that gay vibe JB kept getting off him. Rickman was supposed to be Mr. Tough-macho straight guy, but that wasn't what JB kept getting. Once the pool area was empty—JB had seen from the corner of his eye Rickman indicate to the other men in the place to scram until it was just the two of them at the table—Rickman started flirting with him. He was what? JB couldn't believe it. The man was coming on to him. He knew what it was since he'd been the recipient of a few passes in his day. Rickman wasn't all that overt, mind you, but it was still a come on. Not well executed either, clumsy and somewhat little boy like. What a kid would do when asking a prom queen out for a date. Frogs in the pockets, pulling pigtails, that kind of thing. It became, after Rickman's first few moves, tedious and irritating. JB didn't care if Officer Terry Rickman was the town's terminator and ninja rolled into one, he was queer. Queer as Elton John on George Michael. And he wanted JB. He ignored it as well as he could and concentrated on playing the pool game.

Finally, when he'd had enough, JB asked when they should meet the next night. He found out Rickman would meet him there at Goldys and take him to the poker game in his car. JB begged off from another game—the man staring at and commenting on his ass was really over the line—and went to talk with Goldy.

"I can't believe it. That man was cruising me, Goldy. I swear to you, he really was."

"Rickman? You must be wrong. He hates gay people."

"Well, he doesn't hate me. I cut him off when his hand touched my ass."

"Rickman? No. He's rumored to have beat the crap out of a gay guy that came through here just last month. There was a whole gang of them and they ran that guy right out of town." Goldy got a worried look on his face. "I'm not so sure you should go to that poker game."

"Why? You don't think they would try to beat me up, do you?" Goldy didn't answer. He simply raised an eyebrow.

"Your kidding?" JB said. "But he was cruising me over there. Do you believe that? The man was trying to put the moves on me. And he's supposed to be straight. But, you know, I learned a long time ago that no man is always what he appears. Kinsey grossly under-estimated at ten percent. That's why Howard was looking into a gay sex club here in town. You heard anything about that Goldy?"

"The only club I know of is the one you're going to. And nobody knows what goes on at the meetings. The Poker Guys is just a boy's club. Very high school, with secret passwords and handshakes. Baby stuff. But a few people...and they're damn few...have been invited to one of their games. And they all refuse to say what went on after. They get real closed mouthed. Even Eddie Falco wouldn't say anything. And he's got the biggest mouth in town."

"He did in high school too. He always was a snitch." Eddie was still sitting at the other end of the bar. "I'll have to talk with him and see what I can find out. Give me another beer and one of what he's having."

JB walked down the bar and sat next to Eddie. "So, Eddie, thanks for the introduction to Rickman. It got me invited to the poker game." Goldy put their drinks down in front of them.

"On me," JB said. "Eddie, I need you to tell me about this Poker Guys thing. What do you know about it? You've been to one of the games."

"I can't. They swear you to secrecy. And you don't mess with them. They're all hard asses. They'd beat the crap out of me if I told."

"Told what, Eddie? What goes on there?"

"You'll find out tomorrow." He grabbed his drink, downed it, and said, "I got to go, JB. I got an appointment." He was off the stool and out the door before JB could get anymore from him. That's weird, JB thought. Eddie was always a talkative weasel. He turned back to the bar. "Goldy," he called. "Tell me more about this. And about the cop that got killed."

"Well, Vince Barkley was a bad one. He and Rickman were twins in that respect. Arrogant and nasty, both of them. Vince was always throwing his weight around. His being a cop gave him power and he enjoyed using it. Like a big club that he beat the whole town with. I always wondered what his poor wife had to put up with. He couldn't have been any peach to live around."

"His wife, huh. I'll have to talk to her. What's she like?"

"Long suffering I'd say. Poor Rose, she always looks as if she's about to cry. Or scream."

Len had been right, the cast meeting had been called to get New Wendy ready to go on that night. And to get an interim Princess from the chorus ready as well. Cast changes always caused a disruption to any show's routine. There had been several alterations to the play already; constant line changes, musical numbers put in and taken out, new characters, and there were probably going to be more. Luckily, so far, it had served to bring the cast closer. Show companies, especially when they were out on the road, tended to become like big families. Which could be a good thing, when you consider the closeness and the caring that it brings. But families often were also highly dysfunctional and this show was proving to be no exception. At least if Len's suspicions were right.

Len spent the rest of the day getting various members of the cast aside and asking them what they thought about the accident and the changes to the play. He tried to keep it light and gossipy so they wouldn't suspect what he was really after. That he was asking to decide if any of them could be eliminated as suspects in the sabotage of Sneed and Wendy's gangplank.

It turned out that the majority of the featured players weren't viable as villains after all. None of them would have gained anything substantial from the girl's accident. They all seemed content with the parts they had been cast in, so why would they have done anything? And the one's that might have had a motive all gave him noncommittal or unconcerned answers to his questions, which tended to eliminate them as suspects. Len got a lot of humms, ahhhs, and uhs. So for all his trouble he was left with nothing much to show for it.

When he went further down the cast list, looking at the chorus, there were several of the females that could have been involved. At least they stood to gain something from Wendy's accident. Their prospects for better parts, and better money, improved as the next person moved up to the vacated part. In fact, the young women in the cast, and there were at least twenty of them, could have been used to replace the original Wendy when she was injured. The producers would, naturally, first turn to an understudy, but if she didn't work out, then they would have to find another replacement. That could have been any one of the sopranos in the chorus.

Len decided he would take his questions and move away from featured players to focus on the rest of the cast. It made sense that it was somebody who wanted to move up. All those little actresses playing Indians, mermaids, and the like.

The first person Len needed to talk to about them was the dance captain. He was the person in charge of the chorus— the twenty-women and seven men that made up the pirates, Indians, mermaids, and various other parts in the show. These people were also the chaperones, tutors, dressers, and sundry other functionaries that populate a major production on the road. Len had decided that if there was anyone in the cast who was likely to make trouble it would be one of them. They had the most to gain from another actor's mishap. It could mean a better part for them.

The dance captain's name was Michael and he was an anomaly in musicals. He was a straight dancer. He was also charged with keeping the cast in line—ordering extra rehearsals, keeping them fresh in their parts, even assigning the parts themselves for the secondary actors.

He knocked on Len's dressing room door and stuck his head in. "You wanted to see me, Mr. Matthews?" There was an unwritten separation between the leads and the supporting actors. No animosity mind you, but it meant the supporting cast wasn't part of the character name game played among the rest of the players.

"Yes, Mike," Len said. "Come in. I wanted to ask you a couple of questions. Do you mind?"

"No, I guess not. Is there something wrong? Did any of my people get out of line? Walk on one of your lines maybe?"

"No, no, nothing like that. I was wondering if you could give me an idea of who we're working with? Tell me about the cast."

"All of them?"

"Just the highlights."

"Okay. But, I don't understand why?"

"I'm starting a newsletter. The information, Mike."

"Well, what do you want to know?"

"Tell me about the personalities of the people who are working with us. I want to know who they are. Are they easy to work with? Are they ambitious? Do they like each other? That's what I'm looking for."

"Oh. Well, they're all good people, Mr. Matthews. Like all actors, some have bigger egos than others, but they get along all right. Everybody does their job. It's a good crew."

"The same as at IBM?"

"Sort of. Show business is a job, like any other." He hesitated. "Mr. Matthews, I don't understand what your looking for."

"If I take you in my confidence will you keep it to yourself?"

"Of course."

"I think that we have an overly ambitious actress in our cast. She wants to move up in the show and our Wendy being hurt the other night is part of that plotting to get ahead. So, tell me, who among your singers and dancers is the most hungry for a better part?"

"Uh." he said.

"As if I haven't heard that enough today. For Christ's sake, Mike, I'm not asking you to get anyone fired here. I just need to have an idea of who these people are. If someone is causing accidents it can ruin the show, don't you think?"

"You know I was wondering about that very thing. We all noticed that the girl playing Wendy did seem more clumsy and accident prone than most." He looked thoughtful. "Let's see, any one of the women would kill for a featured part. But it isn't very often that one of them moves out of the chorus. That's the stuff of Broadway myths."

"But it does happen. Carol Haney and Shirley MacLaine come to mind." Years before, when Ms. Haney was staring in *The Pajama Game* she was sick one night and her understudy, Ms. MacLaine took over her part. In the audience was a Hollywood producer and a career was born.

"Once in a lifetime."

"I suppose. But who in our cast might try to make it happen with benefit of accident?"

"Most of them aren't the right types, so they wouldn't be considered. There are a couple. Nancy for one, or Marta. Maybe even Gwen. They always seem to be hoping for the worst, and are happy when it happens. That could be a personality quirk though. There's nobody that I can think of that overtly looks to be an outright bitch on wheels."

"Okay. But, Mike, keep your eyes open, will you? If anything happens let me know. And I'll be talking to some of these people as we go along. Okay?"

"You got it. I hope you find out who it is. I don't like these kinds of disruptions with my cast."

"Nor do I."

Next on Len's list to be talked with was Sneed. He was well known to be the biggest gossip in the entire cast. And he was the one person out of all of them that had managed to cross over between leads and supporting players. He knew all the dirt on everyone—who was sleeping with whom, who was riding high in the bitch-mobile, who was cheating on their diet, who was cheating on their spouse back home. Sneed had all the tittle-tattle Mike had been reluctant to give.

Sneed was also a great big queen who had to go some to straighten it up with Wendy every night. He was a good actor who would soon outgrow the juvenile parts that he so far had made his living from. Len hoped he had a fall back to count on because leading man sure didn't look to be an option for him. He came into Len's dressing room puffing on a cigarette in a holder. Not since Noel Coward. A nascent antique dealer maybe?

"Captain, darling, what can I do for you?" Puff, puff. "I just despair of that little vixen playing Wendy now. Isn't she awful?"

"Rehearsals not going well?"

"Well, she's just such a great big Clydesdale. I mean, she moves with all the grace of a hippo. And she weighs a ton." Puff, puff. "The old Wendy was a sprite compared to her. Is she coming back?" One leg flipped over the other and bounced a couple of times before it settled.

"I'm not very optimistic that she will. You'll have to make the best of it, I suppose. The new girl might get better."

"And The Saint will open it's disco doors to the masses." Puff, puff.

"Anyway, Sneed, what I asked you in for was to have a good old gossip session."

He clapped his hands together. Len expected Tinkerbell to come back to life. "What fun. What dish do you have?"

Gossip was something that Len could enjoy on occasion, but having been the brunt of enough of it to have almost lost his career a year or so before did take some of the edge away. However, Len also knew Sneed wasn't going to give anything without having his pump primed. So, Len was expected to start the ball rolling with a tidbit of his own.

"Nothing major. Did you know that The Countess was drinking again?"

"No. That old lush. I thought she was on the wagon."

"Well, she's controlling it, but she had a drink at lunch today. Only one mind you."

"I'm sure there will be more. Well, that's another disaster waiting to happen. As if this show hasn't been cursed already."

"What do you mean?"

"Well, darling, all the accidents, of course." Puff, puff. "Wendy losing her costumes. Her tripping on that misplaced settee. Props in the wrong place. The poor girl was doomed. And now she's out of the show because of a faulty gangplank?"

"Maybe since New Wendy has the part now she'll have better luck."

"Not with that voice. Don't you think audiences will recognize it? She was Witchy Green after all."

The girl, previously, had been the voice of a character on a well-known children's cartoon show. where she had played a comic witch to perfection. With a song almost every week and well written comedy scripts she was a star for three sitcom seasons. One of her songs had even gone almost to the top of the charts. But she was never seen. Always simply a voice on one of the most popular children shows on the air. This play was her chance to break out, that was if her mother had anything to do with it. And she might have. The mother had been one of Len's most likely suspects up to this point.

"Well, it is a chance for our New Wendy."

"Is that what we're calling her? Delightful. I'll give you

odds that the audience will laugh the first time New Wendy opens her mouth. They'll know that voice in a minute."

"If they do the producers will replace her the very next minute. They take this play very seriously."

"Don't they now. I've even had notes about the way I stand.

"It's the hand on the hip, Sneed."

"Here I am trying to add nuance to the part."

"Standing around like Edna May Oliver isn't nuance, its affectation. Butch it up, kiddo."

He stiffened. "You think? With all the intrigues going on around this show you'd think they would have better things to do than pick on my stance."

"What intrigues?"

"Oh, haven't you heard?"

As one of the leads Len tended to find himself distanced from the day to day interactions of the rest of the cast. That's why he was putting up with Sneed to begin with. "Do tell," he said.

"Well, there's Nancy. She's managed to get laid by every straight male crew member in the company. She can barely stand up, poor girl, and when she does she's bowlegged." Puff, puff. "And Gwen, that slut. She slept with Mike just so she could be the barmaid at the end of Act 1. And its just a walk on, not one line. And then there's Marta. She's having an affair with Grace. I mean, with all the screwing going on I'm surprised we make curtain every night."

"No kidding? But, come on, this happens with every show on the road. Get actors away from home and their libidos will go crazy. They're in their own little place. Never Never Stop Screwing Land. Sex *is* one of their favorite things."

"Well, I'm not getting any. I haven't been laid since New York. I haven't found one person to play with."

"True, the producers did cast a bunch of straight pirates for this show. And all those women. What about the crew?"

"No luck. They aren't interested, not when they've got Nancy. Talk about your Lost Boy. Even the crocodile would look good to me about now."

"Well, I don't think resorting to bestiality would be a good idea. Inter-species sex isn't all it's cracked up to be. But I also don't think you're trying hard enough. I'd bet even the Countess could get laid around here. You must have your gaydar switched off."

"What's that?"

"Gaydar? It's a device that all gay men have in their heads. It starts clanging when a likely prospect comes by. My, you are young aren't you?"

"How about you Captain? Your quite a dish."

"And I'm old enough to be your father."

Then a voice out in the hall called for the actors to gather on stage. Sneed's pass was interrupted.

They headed out of the dressing room.

Notes
From
Home

He pushed the brass button that rang the doorbell of Vince Barkley's house. It was a raspy buzzer instead of a chime. JB had left Goldy's. Since there wasn't anything for him to do until he had to meet his sister for dinner he decided to go see the wife of the murdered man. JB had a couple of questions he wanted to ask.

The house was a one story Craftsman, built back in the twenties and kept in excellent shape. Painted white with dark green trim, it had a concrete porch with rock columns at the corners. Oleander bushes bloomed along the front with an expanse of lawn going to the street.

The door opened and JB got his first look at Mrs. Rose Barkley. Goldy had been right, she did look put upon. Her hair was a dull brown streaked with gray, cut in a serviceable pageboy cap. Her clothing was what they used to call a housedress. Cotton, with a machine embroidered collar and short sleeves. It was dowdy, ill fitting, and not very attractive. She held her mouth in a thin line that slashed across her face. The face was pale, without make-up.

"What can I do for you?" she asked.brusquely She sounded annoyed, as if JB had interrupted her program on the TV that blared from the room behind her. It was some religious program. JB could hear the preacher haranguing his audience even out on the porch.

"Mrs. Barkley?" She nodded. "I'm Jeremy Bent. I was wondering if I could talk with you? About your husband? I'm very sorry about his death, but I was a friend of the man who was being accused of his murder."

"And you don't think he did it? The Chief called. He told me you might be coming by. Come in. I'll try to answer you. If I can."

JB followed her into the living room and stood waiting while she finished listening to the evangelist on the TV. When the program went to a commercial she turned it off, crossed to the couch, and primly sat. "Now, what is it you want to know, Mr. Bent?"

"Are you aware of the circumstances of your husband's death, Ma'am?"

"I know that he was found with a rope around his neck, and his pants were down around his ankles."

"Then you knew he was cheating on you?"

She gave a little snort. "When wasn't he cheating is a better question? But I didn't mind if that's what you want to know? It meant he left me alone." She picked at a piece of flotsam on the arm of the couch, then moved a crocheted doily to cover the spot. "Mr. Bent," she went on. "My husband didn't follow the Lord. His dying means that he'll be in everlasting hell for the rest of eternity. In my opinion that's where he belongs. He was an abusive man, Mr. Bent. He hurt me." She rubbed at her shoulder. "God forgive me, but I'm glad he's dead."

"Do you know who might have wanted him dead?"

"Myself, for one. That doesn't mean I did it though. Most everybody in town didn't like Vince. He had a habit of making people very angry with him. I'm surprised that he wasn't killed sooner."

So much for the grieving widow. Her face was a mask of disapproval. JB didn't think anyone could meet the higher than thou standards she seemed to live by and expected of those around her.

"It could have been anyone. But since it concerned sex. Well, with Vince it usually did. He was a sinner and a degenerate, Mr. Bent. I suggest you go talk to that whore. What's her name? Molly? She's as likely a culprit as the next person."

"Like you, Mrs. Barkley, she claims she didn't do it."

"And you would accept the word of a whore, Mr. Bent? A fallen woman. What makes you think she isn't lying."

Where was she getting this stuff? It sounded like Temperance rhetoric out of another century.

"And what would make me think you aren't lying, Mrs. Barkley?"

She pulled herself up and sat stiffly. "I'm a God-fearing woman, sir. Lying is against the good book. I wouldn't do it." Carrie Nation reincarnated. The only thing missing was a hatchet.

"I would suspect there are quite a few things you don't do, Mrs. Barkley." JB smiled hoping to temper how disapproving that must have sounded.

"I don't drink, or smoke, or put up with nonsense, Mr. Bent. And I wouldn't put up with it from Vince either. Vince Barkley was a perverse and immoral man. The things he wanted me to do I couldn't ever countenance. Why he tried to make me into a scarlett and painted woman just to satisfy his carnal desires. I wouldn't have any truck with that sort of sin. That's why he went to that trollop. She will be as damned as he is. I'm sure she satisfied all his carnal perversitys. I certainly wouldn't."

"I'm sorry, Mrs. Barkley, but a painted woman? I'm afraid I don't understand. Could you explain?"

"He tried to make me dress in a hussy's clothes, Mr. Bent. Silly little tank tops. Ungodly short shorts. And he wanted me to wear garish make-up. Rouge and bright red lipstick. I am not a wanton woman, Mr. Bent."

"I'm sure." Hadn't there been lipstick traces on Vince's body? "The make-up, Mrs. Barkley. Do you still have it?"

"Good Lord, no. I burned it along with the clothes. But I remember the names. The lipstick was called Crafty Crimson. The rouge was Sultry Pink. Slut's wares, Mr. Bent. I put them into the garbage of hell where they belonged."

Rose Barkley was one of those women who condemned and vilified anything or anyone that wasn't on the straight and very narrow path she and her kind stomped like storm troopers. They were an army of accusers. JB was thinking about saying something about being self-righteous and hypocritical when he decided to just leave. She wouldn't change. He couldn't make her. He may as well leave her to her disapproval. She would be standing at the end of the world pointing her finger at all the sinners, himself included, as they fell into the pit she was sure they would be exiled to. He said again how sorry he was about her husband's death, which got him another derisive snort, and he left.

JB decided that with her holier than thou attitude she might actually be a candidate for the murder of her wayfaring husband. She wouldn't be the first fanatic to be driven to murder by what they considered an unredeemed sinner. JB knew she would certainly condemn himself. He fit right in with her idea of a craven transgressor. Gay people have been burnt at stakes for centuries. Like kindling at a weenie roast.

He stopped at the local drug store and asked if they carried the lipstick Mrs. Barkley had mentioned. At first the girl wanted to know a brand name. JB couldn't help her. All he had was the name of the color. When he mentioned that the girl perked up.

"That's from the Madam Helena collection. Here it is." She showed him a full line of cosmetics displayed on a corner of the glass counter. The graphics on the box lids looked to be from another era. A hang-over product out of the fifties. From it she picked out a three inch metal tube. It was gold washed tin with a line of tiny rhinestones around its middle. The color of the lipstick was a flame bright red. When JB held it to his nose it smelled strongly of dying roses.

"Whew. That's a strong smell. Does the whole line smell like this?"

"Yes. It's the trademark for the line. Its been around for ages. There's only a few older ladies that still use it. The lipsticks have their own taste too. Crafty Crimson is supposed to taste like red cherry's. To be honest it tastes like cough drops. *Smith Brothers*, you know? Most other brands of lipsticks have no taste at all, and they usually only smell of wax."

"Do you sell a lot of this stuff?"

"Not really. As I said, only for one or two old ladies. We keep it in stock mostly for one customer. He gets it for his girlfriend."

"Who's the customer?"

"Oh, Officer Barkley. He's a policeman. He gets a tube almost every month. That's sure a lot of lipstick, isn't it? Most women don't use that much in a year. Humm, I guess since he's dead we won't be selling much of this anymore."

"Well, I'll take this tube." He handed over the twenty he'd won from Rickman in their pool match and then had to dig for change. Expensive taste Vince Barkley had.

Molly the Whore's place was an apartment over the local independent hardware store. Most of these single owner stores across America had been closed down by the big warehouse establishments proliferating in most cities. *Home Depot* was cutting a wide swath. Independents couldn't beat the prices and ended up closing because of no business. Only in America.

But not in Peebels. The local hardware store was a gathering place for most of the town's players and toffs. Having Molly upstairs was a definite draw. The wives in town could never figure out why their husbands would suddenly start wanting to do woodworking projects. Bird houses, what-not shelves, and shoeshine boxes proliferated. Some went so far as to build entire additions onto their houses. The town had a long tradition of do-it-yourselfing.

Molly came from a long line of soiled doves. She was a third generation woman of easy virtue. Her mother before her had plied her business to the men of the town, as had Molly's grandmother before that. The dynasty went all the way back to the prairie days and the founding of Peebels proper. The first of that long line of floozies had arrived in the territory a day or two after the first farmers looking for new opportunity. In those days a woman had few of their own opportunities. School teaching, laundress, and whore was about it; and lying on your back was easier than scrubbing dirty longjohns and wrangling recalcitrant youngsters.

JB walked up the stairs and stood on Molly's small landing. There was a traditional red lightbulb in the sconce by the door. She probably got a discount on them from the store downstairs. He knocked. He could hear some scuffling around inside and then the door was opened.

Molly was about Sara's age. Twenty-five, maybe twenty-seven. But she looked hard. Heavy foundation on her round face, tosseled bed-head dark hair, and exotic eye make-up. Like what Elizabeth Taylor wore as *Cleopatra* back in the 60's. And she was maybe ten or fifteen pounds overweight, still shapely, but going to fat. She was dressed in a cotton flower printed full length robe tied at the waist.

"What can I do for you, stud?" she said.

"I was wondering..."

"Well, you don't have to wonder anymore, baby. Yes, I'm available. And, yes, I put out."

"Good to know," JB said. "But that isn't why I'm here. I'm Jeremy Bent, and I wanted to ask a few questions about Vince Barkley."

"I already talked to the Chief. But I'll answer your

questions, sweetie. For a price."

"How much?"

"Whatta ya got?"

"How about twenty? Do you take travelers checks?"

"Honey, I take *Visa* and *MasterCard*. Hell, I'll even validate your parking."

"Then its a yes?"

"Sure. Why not? Come on in."

She stepped aside and JB went through the door.

Inside was a bedsitter apartment. A two toned striped wallpaper in the front room with an efficiency kitchen on the left. There was a curtained area at the back with an iron posted bed, nightstands, and lamps. The lamps were in the shape of women dressed in full length frilly lace dresses. The bed was unmade.

Molly went over to the couch, made herself comfortable, and lit a cigarette. She blew out the noxious smoke and said, "So, whatta ya want to know?"

JB sat in the overstuffed chair opposite her, "I was going to ask about Vince Barkley. He was found with lipstick traces on his body that indicated that he might have been having sex with a woman when he was killed. Were you that woman? His wife says it wasn't her. And I believe her."

"Don't blame ya. She looks like she could be the most uptight in a town full of uptight prigs. But, like I told the Chief, Vince wasn't one of my regulars. So, I wasn't with him that night. Or ever. He didn't came near me anymore. He used to visit, a couple of years ago, but that stopped. What I'm getting at is if he was with a woman, it probably was some housewife from around here, although I can't imagine who. Might have been someone from out of town. I know it weren't me. Besides, I don't own a car, so I couldn't have driven out to the bridge to begin with."

"No car? How do you get around?"

"I don't. Most any place I need to go is within walking distance in this burg, and my johns or my brother will usually bring me whatever I need. I have regulars that do favors for me. Thank God. As small as this shithole is I barely get by. I'm even thinking of quitting the life. Find me something legit to do. Hooking don't make for a great living in these small towns."

In New York, an escort could usually be guaranteed about two hundred and up for an evening. Here, JB supposed, Molly had to subsist on twenty to forty dollars a trick. It had to be tough getting by.

"You said Vince used to come to you. Why did he stop?"

She tapped her cigarette on the edge of a cheap metal ashtray. "I'm pretty easy most of the time. Hell, I don't care if a guy wants a feather up his ass, like Yankee Doodle. But, there are limits to what I'm willing to do. Vince wanted me to do some stuff that I didn't want to get involved in."

"Like what?"

"Have you ever heard of erotic asphyxiation?"

"Yeah, I have heard of it. Its called scarfing isn't it? Sure. So, Vince was into that?"

"Big time. It's a dangerous game. People have died. I read about that actor. What was his name? Albert somebody? Dekker?"

JB nodded. Albert Dekker had been a popular movie character actor back in the 40's. He was found dead in his Hollywood apartment in 1968. He was wearing lipstick, a pink silk nightie, and a rope around his neck. He was hanging from a ceiling joist, a tipped over chair under his nylon stocking clad feet, his underwear at his ankles.

Molly sniffed, "I refused to play with him. Vince took his toys and went someplace else for his games. I didn't mind losing him as a john. He wasn't very nice. He liked to beat up on women. I had bruises. And that stupid fetish of his."

"What was that?"

"Oh, he always wanted me to wear this particular lipstick color. It was awful. Bright red, like out of the 50's. An ugly color."

JB held out the tube from his pocket. "Is this it?"

She opened it and looked. "Yeah, that's it." She held it to her nose, then handed it back to him. "Don't it smell something terrible? Well, Vince always insisted that I wear that shit. Said it was a turn-on. It reminded him of his first lay. Go figure?"

"Yeah, I had a guy once that wanted me to wear argyle socks and brown loafers. He had drawers full of socks in all kinds of colors. Although, I did get a new pair of *Bass Weegin's* from him."

"A guy? So you play for the other team?"

"That I do, Molly. I'm both the pitcher and umpire rolled into one."

"Ya ever tried playing on my side of the field? I could cure ya, big guy. How about we give it a go?" She let the sleeve of her robe fall from her shoulder showing she was naked underneath.

"Well, to cure someone, they have to have a disease. I don't consider being gay a malady. I'm not sick, so there's nothing to cure. Although I appreciate the offer, I think I'll stick with the team I enjoy, thank you."

"Its a shame though. I could give you quite a ride."

"I'm sure you could. But I'd rather have the batter, not the catcher."

Molly's revelations cleared up several questions JB had about this cop killing he was looking into. First the killer had to have a car. That put Molly in the clear. Of course, it opened up the field to anybody else in town that did have transportation. And pickup trucks were a number one consumer product in these environs. Also, considering how people seemed to feel about Vince that made for a whole lot of suspects. The auto-scarfing/asphyxiation thing was interesting. It explained why Vince was found in the condition he was. His killer took advantage of Vince's vulnerable position and so was able to overpower him and strangle him with his own rope. To overpower someone as strong as Vince reportedly was would take some real strength on the killers part. Could a woman have managed that? A man certainly could. But would a man put up with the lipstick fetish? It wasn't unheard of for a man to wear lipstick. Look at any drag queen from here to San Francisco. Were there drag queens in Peebels? How about Goldy? He was outrageous enough to go along with wearing garish lip gloss. But what did he have against Vince? He had no motive. Howard was gay, and might even have worn lipstick, but JB didn't think so. It was totally out of character for him. No, Howard was too butch to do it. So who? It was obvious there was some more investigating JB needed to do before an answer would be available.

After talking with Molly, JB headed back to his hotel. He had a few hours before he was to meet his sister so he thought he should put the time to good use by working on his galley's.

He got in about five pages when the phone rang. It scared the hell out of him. Who could be calling? In the middle of the afternoon? No one knew he was there except Sara and Shirley. Maybe Sara wanted to cancel?

JB picked it up. It was Len. Of all people.

Len had finally tracked JB down by first calling his editor at his publishing house. She told him JB had an emergency in his hometown and had flown out a day or so before.

That was worrying. JB and his family had a contentious relationship at best. Actually, Len got along better with JB's mother than JB did. She had turned her back on him when he came out, and JB didn't forgive easily. So, they weren't the best of friends, but it would be bad for him if she was in trouble. Sick or something.

Len had the number in his book for the cab business JB's sister ran and tried there first. He figured if he could speak to her she could fill him in on what was going on.

It turned out it wasn't JB's mother but some old friend of JB's that was in trouble. Sara told Len JB was at the hotel and gave him that number. Since the cast was still on a break he went ahead and called the hotel in Peebels.

"So you think you're a great detective, JB? Hell, I Sherlocked your ass like a pro, mon friend. I found you like a beagle after a fox. An S after his M."

"I have to admit I am surprised you found me. But why? Is the show OK? They haven't closed and abandoned you in the wilds of the Western frontier have they?"

"That hasn't happened since Lilly Langtry was on tour in 1886. No, there are some things happening that I wanted you to help me with."

"Like what?"

"Not so fast, buddy boy, first we talk about you and your mother."

"How do you know about that?"

"I talked to your sister. She told me."

"Well, I'm going to have to talk with her about telling stories out of school."

"That's not the point. Your mother is."

"Which is a conundrum for the stars."

"Well, I'm the nominal star of this show I'm playing in, will that do? I want to talk about this."

"If you insist."

"Good. Now what's going on?"

"All I know is the last time I called home she refused to talk with me. Now what kind of sense does that make?"

"I must say I have to agree with you. So, my next question is...what did you do?"

"Me? Hell, she's the one who won't talk. I haven't done anything that I know of. Perhaps I gaily exist, therefore I make her angry? Knowing my mother that's a possibility."

"JB, you have to apologize."

"For what? Because I live? Because I'm gay? That I will not apologize for."

"Because she's your mother."

JB made a derisive noise.

"She's the only mother you have, JB. Besides, you may not have her for much longer. You know mine was gone way too soon. Isn't that sufficient reason?"

"I hate it when you do this."

"What?"

"Make sense. You're supposed to be the silly queen in this relationship. I don't like it when you start being wise. All right, I'll talk to her and find out the problem."

"If you don't, no one else will."

"There you go again. Now stop it."

"Righto, matey. Sorry. The pirate I'm playing in this show gets to me every once in a while."

"As long as you don't start hanging out under lampposts looking for treasure and priate booty. Now, what's going on with the show?"

"Ahhh, now that's interesting. There's been a series of accidents, JB. People are getting hurt, and I need to figure out who's doing it."

"What kind of accidents. You haven't been injured have you?"

"Not me, but there's an ingénue that won't be in the show anymore. She had an unplanned fall at the other nights performance."

"You mean somebody else planned it for her?"

"That's what I think. But why?"

"You know all about *All About Eve* don't you?"

"I had thought of that. It's possible."

"I suggest you start talking to the people involved. That's what I'm doing here."

"There?"

"Right. I'm questioning people here in town to find out if they were involved in this mess with Howard. You should do the same."

"Gather the usual suspects from all over Casablanca, right, Captain Renault?"

"Exactly. But there are a few other questions I need answers too..." JB went on to explain the story about Sara and Shirley he had found in Howard's notes.

"So Sara's gay?"

"That's what I think Howard was intimating."

"A hell of a family you got there, sport."

"What am I supposed to do with this? Now that Howard is gone I can't verify the story. Should I confront them? I can't believe they didn't think I'd understand."

"JB, remember where they live. Aren't there cross streets called Murder and Homophobia in that town? You said men with nooses patrol at night. Closets are long established and built to last. What else would two lesbian's do in that atmosphere?"

"I suppose..." JB hesitated. "No, it isn't right, Len. Two people in love shouldn't be something to be hidden. Hell, We should celebrate it. Two choruses of *You Must Remember This* are what's called for."

"Romantic as hell, aren't you?" Len began to quote from the movie, "You played it for her. So you can play it for me. Play it, Sam." Was that Bogart or Bergman? Len would leave it for

JB to figure out.

JB chuckled. They were back to their usual banter. Familiar territory.

Then Len said, "You know, JB, if Sara and this woman are having an affair they're probably still in the wonder of it all stage. What it actually means to their lives comes later. You should try to help them through it, JB. A knowledgeable warining can't hurt. You get to be the voice of experience. You'll love that, won't you? And no berating them for not telling you. Understanding is what's called for here."

"Understanding what?"

"That they're going through the same pile of crap-olla you went through twenty years ago. That hasn't changed has it? The same fear of disapproval, the same hatred and bigotry. You need to help them, JB."

"Will you stop being so damn smart. What is it that's causing this."

"Actors become their parts, JB. Captain Hook runs a tight ship. And Hook ain't no fraidy-cat. Besides, I have a mystery to solve here."

"Don't we all?"

Notes From Home

At around seven, JB got up from his desk and went in to clean up. He had his dinner with Sara to get to. He drove the cab out to the Old Forks Road and into the parking lot of the restaurant.

Triggers was a family style restaurant and an institution there in town. Opened in the 1940's by the mother of the family, they served the juiciest BBQ for three counties. Their secret sauce had won awards as far away as Texas. Along with the ribs they served the flakiest rolls ever invented. Another secret recipe which depended on 7-Up being added to the batter, the rolls were perfect for sopping up sauce on a plate.

JB wandered into the foyer. The entire place was fixed up as if Yosemite Sam was their interior decorator. Tooled leather and bull horns, gun collections and western paintings, cowhide upholstery and suede fringe. JB spotted Sara sitting at a table in the dining room. He went over to her and bussed her cheek.

"Hi, Younger Sister. Have you been waiting long?"

"Not so long, Older Brother. I already ordered for us. Your having ribs, smashed potatoes, and fried Okra. Sound okay?"

"Perfect. Exactly what I would have ordered."

"Good."

The waiter came over. JB asked for a cold beer.

"So, Sara, how's things?"

"Things are screwed, JB. I was talking with Ma."

"Yeah? What's up with her anyway? I got a call from Len this afternoon and he's as perplexed as I am. He said you told him there were problems between us. Why did you do that? It wasn't any of his business. So now I have him on my back trying to smooth things out."

"I told him because he's one of the few people that can get through to you. I talked to Ma about this rift between you two. She knows you're in town. Now she's hurt that you didn't stay at the house."

"With her angry at me it didn't seem to be such a good idea. I don't want to get into anything with her, Sara."

"Well, I found out why she's so angry. It's because she feels left out."

"Out? Out of what?"

"Your life, JB. She's only found out recently that you and Len aren't together anymore. It was two years ago you two broke up. And you didn't think to tell her? She's very upset. And she didn't know anything about Toby either, or that you were out dating again."

JB was caught. He had to admit it, he did tend to keep his mother in the dark as to his personal life back in New York. It also dawned on him that maybe it was a deeply ingrained family trait, keeping upsetting news to themselves. Sara's keeping her affair with Shirley to herself maybe was what she thought was expected by the family. JB had to admit he did it. Sure, he knew Sara was okay with his lifestyle, so she usually got the news, but his mother...not so much. JB was well aware his being gay was still a sore point with his mother. Even after all these years it was something she wasn't totally comfortable with. So he chose not to rub her nose in it. If she had asked he would have gladly filled her in. But she didn't, so he didn't. They talked around it, not about it. His mother got the headlines not the in-depth report.

"Well, Sara, I didn't want her to worry. My love life is my own business anyway. Exactly like yours is if you choose to keep it that way. You know about Len. He was drinking heavily then. I couldn't live with him like that. So we broke up. It happens. He's still in my life. Good God, how could he not be? We live in the same building. We're close friends. We just don't live together. Anyway, Len's out on the road right now. And Toby? Well, that was a very short lived affair. It didn't work out. Now he's out in LaLa land. Hollywood has their hooks in him. Do you tell mother every detail about who you're dating?"

"Who I'm dating isn't the point. Ma feels like she's lost you, JB. She knows you ran away from here to live in New York, and she blames herself. It bothers her."

"Well, I can guarantee you that I'm not coming back here only because she feels guilty about being a bigot. I assume she hasn't changed in that respect? I've made my peace with it, so should we all."

"Hello."

They looked up. Shirley was standing at the table.

"Shirley. What are you doing here?" Sara's acting talents didn't extend to fooling JB. This was planned. "Why don't you join us?"

"If JB doesn't mind?"

"Of course not. Sit, Shirley. We're running into each other all over the place aren't we? Almost like in-laws, huh?"

Sara coughed on the sip of water she was taking. She set the glass down. "JB, why don't you tell us what you've found out about Howard's case. I'm sure Shirl would be interested."

JB went on to tell them what he had so far discovered about Howard's involvement in Vince Barkley's death, and what he had accomplished in pursuit of some answers. "So I'm going to this Poker Guys thing tomorrow night. I'm curious to find out if it's the gay underground club Howard was writing about. It look's like there's all kinds of gay activity in this town." JB gave both Sara and Shirley a meaningful look. "Who'd have thought? Oh, and I've made some sense out of the strangulation angle of the killing too..." He explained about the asphyxiation sex game and how Barkley was caught in the position he was in. "So, I've been able to figure out how he was killed. Why is the question now? I'm also not comfortable with suicide as the explanation for Howard's death. It doesn't feel right."

"Speaking of that," Shirley said. "I need another favor from you, JB. Could you be at the funeral home tomorrow to help me with Howard's arrangements."

"What's wrong with your Mother? Vivian should be doing that, shouldn't she?"

"Mother is totally incapacitated. She's so devastated over Howard's death that she's taken to her bed and won't leave. I can't do this alone, JB. Could you help with the arrangements?"

Sara said, "You will, won't you, Older Brother?"

"I suppose I can. But its making it hard for me to

get any of my own work done. I still have those galley's to get corrected. Remember?" JB sighed. "What time should I meet you, Shirley?"

"You are a good person, Older Brother."

"At ten AM."

"And you are a giant nooge, Younger Sister. I'll be there."

The waiter brought two plates of ribs, helped Sara and JB into their beef bibs—which were the same as lobster bibs but grilled and braised—then took Shirley's order for her dinner.

"Eat, both of you. Don't let your food get cold. Mine will be here shortly." She took a sip of water and reached for a roll.

JB and Sara dug in.

After a few bites, JB decided to do some digging in the gay gardens. "So how about that Lilly Tomlin?" he asked. "She's on Broadway now with her play. *Signs of Intelligent Life.*"

Sara said, "You'd know more about that, JB. You live there."

Okay, so theatre wasn't going to ba a viable subject. How about literature?

"So have you two read *The Well Of Loneliness*?"

The two women looked at JB like he was crazy.

Movies then?

"Hey, have you seen *Desert Hearts* yet? It's supposed to be good."

Sports?

"How about that Martina? Hell, of a tennis player, huh?"

"JB, will you stop it. What are you going on about?"

"Good God, I guess I'll have to spell it out. L-e-s-b-i-a-n. Sara, are you and Shirley together?" They looked at each other. "As lovers?"

"How could you possibly know?"

"Then you are? Howard left a story about you. I wasn't sure if it was fiction or true life. Why didn't you think you could tell me? Of all people."

"We haven't told anyone. I don't even know how Howard knew."

"Probably from you spending all your time together. Even I was getting suspicious, and I got into town yesterday. You know you should tell. Come out, come out, as the Munchkins of Oz say so eloquently."

"JB," Sara said. "Do you remember what it was like when you came out? Well, Peebels hasn't changed."

"Since I got here, what a day ago, I've seen at least two

people who are out and gay...now that's four if I count you two.
Also, I've found out about an underground gay sex club. And,
to top it off, I was accepted by what's supposed to be the town's
primary homophobe. Who I don't believe is as homophobic as
he puts on, but that's beside the point. Peebels hasn't changed?
You've got to be kidding? It's beginning to look like the Sodom of
the Plains around here. Pass me the salt will you, Mrs. Lot."

"How do you think Mother will react?"

"Sara, you can't live your life dependent on what a bigoted
parent thinks. I've been out for almost twenty-three years and I
can honestly say that I only regret perhaps three days in all that
time. I've had to fight for what and who I am. And I've learned to
take pride in the world I live in. And I couldn't have done it any
other way than the road I took to get where I am today. Believe
me, Sara, you have to be true to yourself. You can't be happy
living a lie. Besides, although she's doing it grudgingly, Mother
has begun to accept my lifestyle. For her that's a big deal."

Shirley reached over and took Sara's hand. "Maybe he's
right?"

"I am. Especially now, when so many of our kind are dying
from this plague that's afflicting us. We need to be visible to prove
to everyone that we aren't a small minority that doesn't care. We
need to show the world that we're a community and that if we
have to, if they won't, then we'll take care of our own. If the rest
of the world has no compassion for us then we have to provide it
ourselves. We'll have to be our own caregivers, our own support
group. And that means we have to be out there showing the
world we care, getting medical people to help, making medicines
available, giving this disease a face. We need all the help we can
muster. Don't turn your back on your own kind, Sara."

"We're two women in a small town, JB."

"It only takes one to make a difference. Larry Kramer, in
New York, started a group called the Gay Mens Health Crisis,
GMHC for short, back in 1981 all by himself. Now its spread all
over the country. Groups have sprung up everywhere in response
to AIDS. It only takes one, Sara." JB looked at Shirley, then back
at Sara. "Okay, maybe two. One to help the other."

"But what can we do?"

"You can start by coming out. Simply being visible is
considered a political act these days."

$\mathcal{S}$need had been right.

When New Wendy uttered her first line, "Why have you stolen me good sir?", the audience started to titter. As she continued her nerves got the better of her, with the result that her voice rose in its pitch. She sounded more and more like her cartoon self as she went along. Witchy Green was on her broom for all to hear. So it wasn't a surprise when the audience started to laugh at every line she said. The lines weren't funny, and they weren't written so they would be, but that recognizable cartoon voice certainly amused the audience no end. By the time she got to her first song it was a train wreck. And it went like that for the rest of the performance.

At the interval, Len found New Wendy sitting on the stairs to the upstairs dressing rooms crying her eyes out. He went to her. Len had found himself placed in the position of being a sort of father figure to the kids in the show. He sat beside her. He wasn't sure what he could say to make her feel better, but he had to try something. "My dear, now stop, you mustn't take it so seriously. It's only a play."

"Tell Mummy that," she wailed "She's blaming me for this. I can't help it if they all know my voice. How am I supposed to change it?" When she had played the Indian Princess, she had lowered the pitch of her voice. And since her lines were mostly ughs and gestures it hadn't sounded quite so familiar.

Now, however, as Wendy her voice was going into that higher register and audiences roared every time they heard it.

"Perhaps if you lowered the tone of your voice?"

"I can't," she wailed again. "I get so nervous, especially when they start laughing, and it goes all squeaky on me. God, how I hate acting. I wish I wasn't even in this awful predicament. But Mummy won't let me get out of the show. All I want to do is go back home and live like a normal kid."

"Well, by your next birthday you'll be able to decide that for yourself. No matter what your mother says, you'll be eighteen then and you can make your own decisions."

"Oh, that's not for years yet...," she said. Then she stopped. The look on her face clearly indicated she had said too much. And she couldn't pull it back. She tried, badly, to cover. "I mean, yes, I will won't I." A false smile crossed her face. Her eyes, however, were fearful. "But I don't know what I'm going to do right now. What do you think I should do, Captain?"

"Well, you're in the part now so you'll have to keep playing. Until the director and the producers make some sort of decision you'll have to keep going on. That's the most professional thing to do. After they do decide then you'll know if you can go home or not. Where is that anyway?"

"What?"

"Your home? Where were you born?"

"Oh, in Indiana. A town called Shelbyville. But now we have a house out on Staten Island. Mummy wanted us to be closer to Broadway. I wish I was back on the island."

"I'll tell you what. I'll talk to the Croc and see what his plans are. Then I can let you know." Len had a pretty good idea what the Croc would say. New Wendy was surely going to be replaced. At least that would let her out of her misery. "But for now we still have another act to do. Can you stand it? I know all of us will help as much as we can."

"I will. And thank you, Captain." She stood and started up the stairs. That's when Sneed came by. 'Stop, there," Len said to him. "You too young lady." She came back down the stairs. "Sneed, I want you to do something for me, okay? I want you to hold on to this girl's hand throughout the rest of the play, except when she's on stage, of course. I want you to be her rock. You need to be a steadying influence for her. And, you my girl, I want you to concentrate on getting your voice out of the clouds and back where you mean to play it. Don't worry about acting, only pay attention to the quality of your voice."

New Wendy was standing next to Sneed. He held out his hand. She put hers into his. He smiled and said, "Come on, girl, let's wow them. Whatta you say?" She nodded shyly.

"That's fine," Len said, then added, "Sneed, when the show's over would you come to my dressing room? I want to speak with you."

"Sure."

Sneed took New Wendy over by the side curtains so he could work with her. Help her to get her voice under control. Len went on to his dressing room. He wanted to talk to the long distance operator about a phone number.

New Wendy's slip that she had years to go before she was of age had intrigued Len. Just how old was she anyway? She had seemed young from the very beginning, back when she was first cast in New York. But her mother insisted she was seventeen. Len now had his doubts. It wouldn't be the first time a stage mother had faked her kids age to get a part for her. Ann Miller was only 14 when she started in the movies. She said she was 18 and got away with it. Joan Blondell was younger than her reported years too. The Gerry Society watched kids in vaudeville back then and being underage would get them thrown out of their jobs. So they lied. Besides, kids today all looked like they were older instead of younger. That was TV's influence.

Len got from information the number for the county clerk's office in Shelbyville, Indiana. He would call them first chance he had. Then he would know for sure if New Wendy was more a minor than presented by her parent.

The show rolled along toward its curtain. New Wendy, with encouragement, did manage to get her voice more under control. She sounded better and the laughs were less. That meant a stronger show. It also made the other actors jobs easier. One character who throws a performance can effect every other cast member. Timing is off. Lines are missed. Cues aren't picked up. It makes the actors generate enough flop sweat to drive the show to ruin. It can get you fired.

Funeral homes were the same as jails in JB's book. Whether here or in New York he had visited far too many to feel comfortable in any of them. He'd had to make arrangements for too many of his friends back in the city already. The main difference was in New York they supplied yarmulkes. In Kansas they gave you paper fans.

Deleboy and Son was a converted Mansard style house that had been on the corner of Main Street and State Avenue for eighty years. It was currently owned by the only undertaker in town. Started by George Deleboy back in the 1940's, the funeral home was being run now by Daniel, the son of the business title. Daniel had been a year behind Howard and JB in school. They had always called him Danny Deathboy back then. He now was tall, thin to the point of cadaverous—which was appropriate to his profession—and wore thick glasses that he had trouble keeping on his nose. He was constantly pushing them back up.

Shirley and JB had met outside the house, and were now sitting in Danny's office looking at pictures of coffins.

"Take a look at the rosewood and silver model. It's our most popular and has served well for this kind of ceremony," Danny said.

"Uh, Shirley," JB said. "Howard and I discussed this years

ago. I don't think he'd changed his mind since. He didn't want anything fancy. Cremation and spread his ashes out at the lake was what he said he wanted." He took hold of her hand to help keep her under control.

Shirley looked over at Danny. "That sounds like Howard. Then that's what we'll do."

"Well, you'll still want a service. That will require having the remains on view."

"True, but let's find something presentable and not so expensive. I don't think Howard would mind."

"Fine. Shirley, let's go out to the showroom. I think I have exactly what you're looking for." He stood and went to the door. "Do you want to come too, JB?"

"Well, I was wondering if I could have a moment with Howard. To say good-bye."

"He is here now. Downstairs. But we haven't had time to prepare the remains yet."

"That's not a problem, Danny. I've seen corpses before. Fixed and unfixed."

"According to your last book, you've even seen them at the time of conception."

"You read my book? Then you know that I'm not squeamish around this sort of thing."

Danny nodded and said, "If Shirley says its okay, then I have no objection." He turned to look at her. She nodded her approval, and Danny went back to his desk. He picked up his phone and buzzed the prep room. A few minutes later a young woman came to the office and escorted JB downstairs.

Howard was laid out on a metal table, naked with a folded sheet covering his private parts. His color was a waxy pale yellow, his hair was uncombed, and his expression in death was a peaceful one. He had a slight smile on his face, a shadow of his usual disposition. Plastic tubes ran into and out of his body. Formaldehyde going in, his blood going out. Then he would be cosmetically made up, dressed, and made presentable.

JB went over to the table and looked down. What a shame, he thought. Way too early for death to take him.

The young lady said, "After he's fixed up he'll look better. All the bruising will be covered up."

"Does he have to be embalmed? He's being cremated."

"State law requires it. And he'll need it for the viewing."

"Right."

He looked back at Howard. As his eyes wandered over

Howard's corpse JB noticed his hands. There were scrapes on the knuckles, and dried blood around the nails. Higher up, at his neck, the sheet that had been used for his hanging had left dark purplish bruising behind. Then JB looked closer. There was a second set of bruises on his neck. One set, from the sheet, had left marks that went around and up behind his ears. That tied in with his position when hung. The second bruising was lower. It was an even three-quarters of an inch wide all the way around his neck. It went straight around to the back of his head at the base of his spine.

Well, that isn't right, JB thought. The two sets of marks indicated clearly to him that Howard hadn't killed himself as the Chief would have them believe. Therefore, the scrapes on his hands were probably defensive. Howard had tried to fight off whoever had put the first strangulation device—be it a rope or a belt or a garrote—around his neck. That second bruise certainly didn't set with him hanging himself. To get that mark he must have been strangled with something first. From behind. After he was already dead he was hung from the library ceiling. That caused the second bruise. The two bruises proved Howard had been murdered and set up to look like a suicide.

"Uh, Miss, you need to get Danny down here. And you need to call the Chief and get him over here too. There's something not right about this body."

The Chief arrived about forty-five minutes later with a young man who turned out to be the coroner's assistant.

"Now what's this bruising you're talking about, JB?" the Chief asked.

"It's like I suspected. Howard didn't kill himself. He was hung in the library and made to look like it was a suicide. It wasn't."

The assistant had been examining Howard's body. "He's right, Chief. These marks are consistent with his theory. Strangled first, then hung."

"Well, why didn't you find them before?"

"The second bruises didn't show until later. The embalming fluids will bring out bruises that weren't readily seen before. That often happens, especially when its a hanging. The blood sinks to the lower part of the body. When the body is cut down the blood flows back and the bruises then appear. But since there's no circulation it takes a while for it to happen. So the bruising wouldn't show until after he's been cut down. And the sheet burns look to be post-mortem also. There's a difference in the kind of bruising that a live person gets and one that's dead."

"So this is a murder, right?"

"It looks that way, Chief."

"Damn. Another one. First Barkley, now this."

"I think the two deaths are connected, Chief." JB leaned against the wall and crossed his arms. "Howard being killed is related to Barkley's death somehow. I'm not sure how yet but its there."

"JB, don't you ever stop coming up with theories? I can only go after one case at a time. And Vince Barkley, a good cop, is my main priority right now. The whole force wants this solved too. But, I'll want this body back at the morgue right away. And I want another full autopsy before he's cremated."

The assistant went to the glassed in office and picked up the phone, probably to call his boss. The Chief turned back to JB. "I mean it. I really don't see how Howard getting killed is connected to Barkley's death. One of my cops is dead and I can guarantee you that we'll find out who did it. Now that Fellows is dead..."

"Is it possible that one of the cops in the jailhouse killed Howard? As revenge for killing Barkley?"

A cop killer is the worst kind of scum to the victim's fellow officers. They pull out all the stops to get him. That's true not only in a big city like New York, but even in a small town like Peebels. And revenge by cop against a suspected police killer wasn't unheard of in either city.

"Another theory, for God's sake. But its not likely. There was only one of my men on overnight duty when Howard was in the jail. And only a couple of prisoners."

"Then it has to be one of them. Who else had access? Who was the cop?"

"Terry Rickman."

"Vince's best friend? Are you kidding? Who else would have had a better motive?"

"I won't believe it. Rickman is a good cop. He's been on the force for years and there's never been a sign that he might be crooked. He'd never kill someone."

"Chief, you said the same thing about Barkley, and its turning out that he wasn't such a straight arrow after all. What you as the Chief see, and what the reality is look to be totally different things. You need to do some investigating of your force I think. At the least, all the evidence points to Howard's murderer being someone that was in the jail the night he was killed. So you should question them about it. That makes sense doesn't it?"

"I suppose. But, hell, I wouldn't have the least idea of what to ask. Do you think you could do the questioning? It's your theory so you'd know what we would need to know."

"I could. But I'd have to check out their records first. I want to know if there's any connection with Barkley. Can we go to the station?"

"Sure. My man will be here soon with the meat-wagon to pick up Fellows. We can go on ahead. I'll leave the assistant here to watch over him."

Driving to the Chief's office took JB through Peebels streets that looked both familiar and not quite so familiar to him.. Houses on streets he had walked as a child were now painted different colors. Storefronts he had spent his allowance in were now closed or contained different business. Saplings had become trees. His town had changed and it was no longer his. JB's hometown was now New York City and he longed to get back to it.

However, he couldn't do that until the murder charge against Howard's good name was dropped and gone. He also needed to know who had killed Vince. The two killings, Vince's and Howard's, would not be left unsolved before JB left town. His conscience couldn't let him abandon the search. Plus, the Chief wanting him to help remove the cases from his books didn't hurt either. JB was loath to admit it, but his ego had swelled a little at being asked to help, especially when the ask-ee was a man who was sure he would end up having his own criminal record when he was a kid. Instead here JB was working at clearing two major crimes from the Chief's books. Fate works ever strange.

At the office JB first went to the computer that sat on its own desk in the bullpen.

"Are you sure you know how to work that?" The Chief hovered

over him. "We just got it a year ago. I only have one man here in the office that can use it so far."

"I've been writing on a computer at home for several months now," JB said. "And before that I was using a word processor. These things are going to take over the world some day soon, Chief."

"Well, be careful. That's a two-thousand dollar machine."

"Uh, Chief, its asking for the password. Do you know it?"

"Wait a minute." He wandered off to find Jess, the clerk.

JB sat waiting. He was also contemplating some of the stuff that was going on. Vince, he knew, must have had some connection to whoever had killed Howard. That he was sure of. But proving it might be the difficult part. JB wondered if Vince had kept notes? Most cops he knew kept a notebook or something with reminders for when they had to go to court for testimony. If Vince had kept notebooks it could go a long way toward making a case that he had some involvement in Howard's getting killed. Maybe he'd kept his notes in his locker there at the station. The locker room was across from the pen JB was sitting in. He could see them lined up through the row of windows on that side of the room. Metal gym style lockers painted a police blue with yellow frames around the edges.

He got up and tried to look like he belonged there as he walked over to the door. There were names in black marker written on white medical tape stuck to the fronts of each of the lockers. Barkley's was the third over. There wasn't a lock hanging off the handle so JB feared the worst. He opened it and found it empty. What had happened to his stuff, JB wondered? The Chief stuck his head into the room.

"What are you up to, JB?"

"What? Oh. I was thinking there might be some information among Barkley's stuff. But there's nothing here."

"That's because we sent his effects over to Rose, his wife. Anything that was here is at her place. I got the password, JB. Let's get going. Okay?"

JB went back to the computer and used the code to open up the Peebels police current prisoner files.

There were three inmates in the jail the night Howard was killed, and one cop. Officer Rickman was going to be easy to find. JB had an appointment to meet him that evening for the Poker Guys game.

The prisoners all were still being held in the jail, and it turned out each of them had some connection to Barkley. The

drunk, JB was surprised to see, was Theodore Amos. Mr. Amos
had been his freshman gym teacher back in high school. JB
had had a huge crush on the man. What had brought Mr.
Amos to this, he wondered? Drunk and disorderly at one of the
local gin mills. Besides Goldy's, booze was a major business
venture in Peebels. There were at least seven other bars spread
around town. It looked like Mr. Amos had been eighty-sixed
from all of them. Barkley had arrested Mr. Amos the night
before he died, that was on a Friday. He'd put him in the tank
and let him sleep it off until he could go to Monday's court
for the umpteenth time. In court the judge had sentenced
Mr. Amos to ninty days. He was on day three of the sentence.

The second prisoner was a kid named Chuck Finucchi. He
was seventeen and had been charged by Barkley with reckless
endangerment. A fancy way of saying he'd been arrested for
hot-rodding out at the old quarry with a bunch of other high
school kids. Chuck was the one that got caught, the others had
managed to get away. He was in jail on a thirty day misdemeanor
charge.

The third person was named Randy Sparks. According to
the computer he wasn't even charged with anything. He was
only being kept in custody. "What's this about?" JB asked the
Chief.

"Sparks is one of Barkley's guys. An informer on that gang
that we're busting for drug peddling. Without his testimony we
don't have a case, so we're keeping him in protective custody
here at the jail. Now that Vince is gone he's more important to
the case than before."

"Is he the one that implicated Howard? Howard told me
someone had said he was involved in selling drugs. Which he
wasn't by the way. He said that was the reason you were out to
find him the night he was arrested."

"As a matter of fact Sparks was the man who fingered
Howard as part of the gang. We put out an arrest order for him
and Rickman found him at the scene of Vince Barkley's killing.
Justice at work, JB."

"It seemed too convenient the first time I heard about it,
and now it seems even more so. I'll want to check into this for
sure. So all of the prisoners had some connection with Vince
Barkley. Then I'll want to talk with each of them. Can that be
arranged?"

"It's my jail. Sure we can arrange it."

"Good. How about right away?"

"Now?" JB nodded. "It'll take me about an hour or so. Can you wait until then?"

"Sure. I have some galleys to correct over at the hotel. Call me when you get it set."

"Will do."

JB walked across the street to the back of the hotel and went up the steps to the nearest elevator.

Once in his room he pulled the galleys from his bag, set them side by side with the manuscript, and dove again into the tedious job of corrections. Before he knew it the call came in from the Chief. That got him up to a whole fifty-four pages of the manuscript. That left two-hundred-eighty-three pages to go. This was going about as fast as a turtle on a treadmill. JB wasn't sure he was going to get the project done in time.

The Chief told JB that the three men were all willing to talk with him and that he could come over at any time. He stretched, washed his face, and took the elevator back down to the main floor. This time through the lobby proper. As he walked across, heading for the back door, he spotted, of all people, his Mother sitting in one of the chairs. He walked over to her. "Mother? What are you doing here? You should have called. Have you been sitting there long?"

She looked basicily the same to him as always. He hadn't been home in three years so there were some changes. Still she looked like what she was. A retired school teacher. She had taught tenth grade English in the Peebels school system for thirty years, until his father died, then she substituted for a few more years after that. She had fully let go of her career only the year before. But she still pulled her now white hair back in its usual bun, and she still wore the wire rimmed glasses that perched on her nose like a bird pecking for food. "I was trying to get up the nerve to call your room, Jeremy," she said. JB still wasn't used to people calling him by his given name. It seemed odd and out of sync. Like he was being reprimanded for some infraction he didn't know he'd broken. And when it came from his Mother the feeling was even more so. "I wasn't sure you would want to see me, Jeremy, not after your last call home. When we didn't speak?"

As if he could forget. "Mother, you should know better. I knew you were put out with me, and I didn't want you more upset." JB took a hard look at her. The changes he did see in her distressed him. She looked tired. The energy that had always lightened her person seemed to have dimmed some. A few of the flashing bulbs that had surrounded her had flickered out. JB guessed Len was right. We really don't get enough time with our parents. It gave him a sad feeling that she was winding down. "So I stayed here at the hotel. I guess I failed. I'm sorry your perturbed with me." JB sat in the chair across from her. "Now, explain to me what it is that has you in such a tizzy." Tizzy? Good God, JB hadn't used that word in eons. Since arks were in vogue. You can try to take the gay guy out of Kansas, etc., etc. "You didn't want to talk with me? What's that about?"

"Jeremy, I found out only last month that you and Len were no longer partners." Mother had always liked Len, even if she didn't want to recognize the two of them had been lovers. "You chose to not tell me that one of the most important relationships you had was over." This was a surprise. She was acknowledging what he and Len had been. Old and growth together as a concept was actually possible. Nice to know.

"Mother, Len and I still are the best of friends, and God knows he isn't out of my life by any stretch of the imagination. We see each other constantly. We even worked together on my last play. My God, I wrote his cabaret act for him. Hell, if we slept in the same bed we couldn't be any closer."

"But, you don't do that, do you? You are seeing other people, Jeremy. And that's what worries me."

"Well, yes. But why should that worry you?"

"Jeremy, we're not totally ignorant of what's happening in the world here in Kansas. If you are seeing other people you could be endangering your very life. Why even that nice Rock Hudson got sick from this disease that is going around now. I don't want that to happen to you, Jeremy."

She was wringing her hands together and seemed to be on the verge of tears. If there was one thing JB could never take that was it. Her crying would make him a puddle in seconds. "Mother, please don't worry. I assure you I am very careful and I don't take chances. Not with my health or my life."

"Now, Jeremy, you're simply trying to reassure me. I've read how you put yourself in the middle of police investigations and such. That's dangerous for you. Why you're even involved in one here, or so I've been told."

"Well, yes, I have become involved in finding out who killed Howard Fellows. How could I not, Mother?"

"I suppose, since you still seem to be enamored of Howard. I never could understand why you were always at his beck and call. He used to order you around like he was the master and you were the hound."

She was right. JB realized that he did let Howard do that to him. JB had been a gawky kid with an inferiority complex. That Howard, the most popular boy in the whole school, was his friend was a very special part of his youth. Because of simply that he owed Howard this. "Its something I have to do, Mother. Try to understand." She nodded. A grudging nod but acceptance nonetheless. "And I finally got to do more of the work I brought with me today. So it'll be all right, I think." He explained that he had brought his galleys to correct, but he didn't think Howard's case would interfere with that deadline.

"Deadline? Oh, dear, didn't I always tell you that you had to meet your responsibilities, Jeremy. You owe your publishers your work on time."

"If its a week or two late they won't stop the publication, Mother. The book will still be on the stands in time for the Christmas holidays."

"Well, I don't approve. And I worry for you."

"Please, don't let it be something else you worry about. I'm fine, Mother, in fact, how about I take you out for dinner while I'm here? Someplace fancy. Then we can have a serious talk. Is it a date?"

"Of course. In fact I have something I wish to tell you too. That would be perfect."

They made plans for the next evening. JB kissed her cheek and they parted. JB understood they would never have the relationship they'd once had. They couldn't be that close ever again. But they could forge something they could both live with.

He went to the newsstand in the lobby and bought a large soda, then back to the rear of the hotel and across the street. The rear of the police station faced the back of the hotel so getting there was quick and easy. He walked the halls until he found the Chief's office and knocked.

The Chief opened the door and without asking him in accompanied JB to one of the interrogation rooms. "I'll have the first man brought in right away," he said. "Who do you want to see first?'

"How about Mr. Amos?"

"Mr. Amos?" The Chief snorted. "He hasn't been anybody but Drunk Ted to everyone around here for years."

"Chief, what happened to him?"

"After his wife and son were killed in a car accident...that was in 1975, I think...he went straight into the bottle. Lost his job at the high school, and has stayed stinking ever since. What's worse is he's a belligerent drunk. Always starting fights and getting into trouble. He's in and out of our jail three or four times a year."

JB shook his head. "That's a shame. I lived with a drunk for a while. It's not a lot of fun."

"Not for the drunk either, I'll wager."

The Chief left. JB sat and waited. In his head he was back twenty-five years. Mr. Amos had been his gym teacher his first year of high school. He had also been the only one to take pity on him, since JB was singularly un-athletic and pathetic at sports.Throw a ball at him and his only reaction was to cringe. As a result Mr. Amos had made him towel boy for his gym period. That meant he didn't have to play, instead he could keep track of the equipment and hand out towels to the boys after they had played their games. For that alone JB worshiped the man. It also didn't hurt that Mr. Amos was one of the first older men—he was all of thirty-three—he got to see naked. That was a definite bonus. Mr. Amos' office was next door to the towel room, and he always showered after class. That afforded JB the chance to watch him when he dried off his muscular body. And he was stunning. Built, in JB's teenage eyes, like a minor god. He was a red head, with light red hair covering that shining freckled white skinned body? And naked! It still affected JB now, years later. He was still a sucker for a redhead.

Mr. Amos was led in by George, and sat across from JB at the table. George looked at JB, looked down at Mr. Amos, shook his head, and went to stand outside the door. As the door clicked shut, Mr. Amos said, "You got a drink, buddy? I need a drink."

His voice was a low mummer and bubbled with the phlegm caught in his throat. And he looked like crap. He was three or four days into a drunk and disorderly sentence, and was in the middle of what looked like a hell of a case of the DT's. Sweat poured off his brow where his now thin hair was pasted flat to his forehead. Any muscle that he once had was wasted away and his scrawny Bags under his eyes actually shook when he moved his head.

shoulders were hunched up around his ears. Four or five days of unshaven beard covered his cheeks. His hair was still red, but now streaked with white. At only fifty-eight he looked like he was seventy and wouldn't have much longer to go if he continued doing what he was doing to himself.

JB slid his soda across the table. "All I have is this. But the sugar will help. You're dehydrated so that will help too." Amos grabbed the bottle and took a big swallow, then coughed to clear his throat.

"Thanks," he said. "I needed that. Whiskey would have been better, but any port you know?"

"Right. And you'll feel better in a day or two. The shakes will stop."

"I hope so. I feel terrible."

"Mr. Amos, do you remember me? I'm Jeremy Bent. I was one of your students."

"There were so many...Bent. That name should be familiar."

JB took it to mean he wasn't as memorable as he had wished. "It doesn't matter. What I wanted to ask you about was what you know about Vince Barkley?'

"Who's that. Was he one of my students too?"

"No, sir. He was the policeman that arrested you. That brought you here."

"Oh, him. What a bastard. A real hard ass. Always after me. Made me miserable. All I want is for everybody to leave me the fuck alone. But he was always getting up in my ass. I hated the prick." Mr. Amos took another sip of the soda and slipped down in his chair.

"Enough to want to kill him?"

"Maybe. But I didn't. I was here when the bastard got it. Sleeping off a bender."

"What about a couple of days later. When the other prisoner was found dead. What can you tell me about that?"

"I heard about that. I was still in the tank. I haven't been feeling too good. I've been puking my guts out. I couldn't even get off the bunk. I feel lousy now as a matter of fact." He grabbed at his stomach. "I get these rolling waves in my gut, like cramps." He moaned and then was quiet.

JB didn't think there was much more he could get from him but asked another question anyway. "Did you know that he was killed, Mr. Amos?"

"Killed? Who? The cop?" He waved his hand. "More the better.

That bastard. Always after me. Up on my ass..."

"No. The prisoner. Howard Fellows didn't hang himself. He was killed."

"Fellows? Was he one of my students? That name is familiar."

Mr. Amos was well on his way to what is called a wet brain. Alcohol will eventually take away your thinking as well as your liver. It was a race to see which went first. JB had heard this already.

"That's all I needed, Mr. Amos. Thanks."

JB stood and went to the door to get George. He came in and took Mr. Amos by the arm.

The old man stood and shuffled beside him. Then he turned back. "Bent. I remember him now. Faggy kid. Lousy at sports. I liked him. He wasn't a complete ignoramus like the rest of those jerks I had to teach."

George took him back to his cell.

JB waited while George locked up Mr. Amos and then brought the kid, Finucchi, to him.

He was just that—a kid. Greasy haired, chubby, baby faced, and small of build. But he walked with a teenage swagger, arrogance dripping off him. Nobody can do smart ass better than a seventeen year old punk. He sat in the chair and swung one leg over the arm. "What's this about?" he said. "The Chief said you wanted to ask about that lousy cop."

"That's right. Vince Barkley was your arresting officer. Maybe you had something to do with his death." That got him. JB noticed a flicker of fear cross his eyes. He was as scared as the rest of us. That swagger was only a thin veneer, his attitude a protective facade. JB could take advantage of that.

"Hey. That's a lie," Finucchi said. "How could I? I was in here. He was killed on a Saturday, right? I was brought in on Friday."

"Well, what makes you think I'm going to believe you?" JB decided to be a little bit of a smart ass himself. "Maybe you got friends that did the deed for you. Are you a gang leader, Finucchi? That car rally you were caught at? Was that a gang thing? Did your gang go after Barkley?"

"What? That's stupid. I ain't no gang leader." His swagger had faded like a ghost in bright light. "Hell, I don't even have any friends. I'm not part of the cool crowd at school, mister. I was only at that rally as a watcher. They wouldn't let me be in it. My car is my dad's Camaro, for crip's sake."

"Why should I believe you? You'd lie so you wouldn't be charged with accessory to murder. What about the guy that was killed in the jail a couple of nights later? You have anything to do with that?"

He shook his head. "Hell, no. I didn't even know the guy. I only saw him here. Reading all the time. He kept to his cell. Even when the door was open and he could have walked around. Instead he stayed in there, his nose in a book."

"So the cells are open in this jail?"

"Sure. During the day. There's a rec area where we play cards and watch TV. And we can go out to the yard or use the library."

"And Howard. That guy. He used the library?"

"All the time. And that day...before he hung himself...he had a visitor in the morning, and then spent the rest of the day in the library. He went in there when he came back and didn't come out. Not even when we locked down for the night. They found him the next morning."

JB had been watching the kid closely. Trying to see if he had any tells. Like in poker, when you have a good hand most people have a tell—a twitch, a gesture, pulling on an ear, for instance, or whistling. Something that indicated when they were holding good cards. When a person lied they often did the same thing. A pulsing vein on their forehead, drumming of fingers, squinting of the eyes, some signal that could indicate to JB if they were being truthful or not. But he did have to look very close sometimes to see it. This kid though, as far as JB could tell, wasn't lying. And George had mentioned earlier that the boy was a joke at his school. But Barkley had, for some reason, a hard-on about him. Vince was always after him. That sounded familar to JB.

"What about Barkley?" JB asked.

"That son of a bitch bastard? He was always bugging me. Hasseling me. For years. I had a run in with him when I was twelve. Caught me setting off a cherry bomb. And he wouldn't let up after that. Drove me bonkers."

JB knew all about that scenario. Chief Rotelli had been his own nemesis years before. "Kid, trust me, I know what that's like."

"Yeah? What did you do about it?"

"Me? I got out of town as soon as I could. I hate to say it, but you should probably think about doing the same. You're still a minor. Anything that happened here is going to be sealed. It won't follow you wherever you might go."

"I could do that. This town stinks anyway."

"Still?"

"But what would I do?"

"I went to New York and found a life for myself. I dropped the small town attitudes, then I used what talent I'd been given and created something out of it. You could do the same."

"But where?"

"Anywhere. Wichita. Topeka. Even New York…if your brave enough."

"You think?"

"Why not? What have you got here? If it isn't Vince Barkley it'll be some other cop. They've hung a tag on you, kid. You're on their books as a troublemaker. That doesn't change. But if you go someplace else you have a chance to begin all over. Reinvent yourself. Be something wonderful."

"I always wanted to sing."

"Then do it. They have clubs in Wichita. Go get a gig in one of them. It would be a start."

"Do you think I could?"

"I think you can do anything you want with your life. And keep in mind that no matter where you end up it's going to be better than here."

The kid went back to his cell with something he didn't have before. Hope. Maybe it would work for him.

JB waited for the last of the prisoners. Randy Sparks. The snitch. He was the one that had put Howard in jail so someone could kill him. JB was sure that if he wasn't the guy that did it then he knew who it had been. That was what JB had to figure out.

Randy came in the room unshackled and in civilian clothes. He didn't wear the usual orange pants and white T-shirt that the other prisoners wore, but was in a pair of gray slacks, with a pink button down shirt. The long sleeves were rolled twice and showed an expensive looking watch on his left wrist and a heavy gold linked chain on his right. He also had a pink fabric belt with a miniature brass military style buckle. The belt's webbing was too long and had been tied around itself so the end of it hung down over his pocket. He had on a pair of brown loafers with pink patterned argyle socks. He looked like he had stepped out of a *Gentleman's Quarterly* spread on what to wear this summer. Even GQ could be wrong. After all, they had endorsed Nehru jackets a few years before. The outfit sat well on a nicely bulked up and muscled body, even if he did look like a raspberry ice cream cone had thrown up on him. George had said that since the man was only in protective custody he was given privileges that a regular prisoner wasn't allowed. His personal goal, JB decided, was to change that status.

Randy sat casually in the chair and crossed his legs, one over the other. A cigarette dangled from his lip. He had dark short spiked hair, and a round face with a strong chin. It was set as if it had been cracked a couple of times. As a result hetended to talk from one side of his mouth. The other side had a palsied look, as if he'd had a stroke somewhere in his thirty or so years. Or maybe he'd been beaten one time too many, because JB could sense that Randy Sparks was well named. Flint like in his demeanor, he was an angry coil ready to spring. The fight vibrated just under the surface of the cool exterior he was so carefully presenting. The man was a trap ready to snap.

"Could you put the cigarette out, please," JB said. "The smoke bothers me." He pushed an ashtray across the table. Randy took a drag, blew it out, and filled the room with more smoke. So that's the way it was going to be? George, who was standing at the open door looking in, ordered. "Put it out, Sparks. Or I'll take em' away from you."

Randy leaned forward and crushed the butt into the ashtray. "All right, for God's sake."

JB asked, "You always like this, or are you trying to prove you're a bad-ass?"

"I am a bad-ass." JB had no choice but to believe him. "Who the hell are you?"

George said, "Watch it, Sparks."

JB said, "Didn't the Chief tell you? I'm the guy that thinks you killed a friend of mine. I'm guessing you're the one who wanted us to think that Howard Fellows killed himself." JB figured that accusing him right off would put him off kilter. Make him panic a little. It didn't. Then again there was a tiny change in the cast of his eyes. Was that fear? Or malevolence?

"What the hell? You're crazy," he said.

"In that case, if I'm crazy, maybe you'll let me do something while I ask a few questions. I want to hold your hand. Would that be okay?"

He laughed. "Hey, what are you? One of the Beatles? You want to hold my hand?" He snorted at his lame joke.

"What I am is a sensitive. I'm like a human lie detector. I can tell by holding your wrist if your lying or not." That was a huge exaggeration but under the circumstances JB felt he could get away with it. "Anyway, you're not my type."

George said, "Don't mess with him, Sparks. I've known him for years. If he says he can tell if your lying, then you should believe him." He winked at JB.

"Yeah. Well, I believe what I can see. Not what some queer tells me. You are queer ain't you?"

"Do you want to know if I'm gay or if I'm British?"

"The same thing in my book."

"I'm what I said, Randy. I tune in to you and know if your lying. It's a power, Randy. Almost like magic. Let me demonstrate. Give me your wrist." JB reached out.

Randy hesitated for a moment then held out his arm. "Sure, what the hell? You think I'm a liar? You'll see."

What JB was going on about was a technique he'd read about in a psych book. An actual lie detector works by measuring heart beats and respiration at specific points on the body. That's what all the wires attached to a subject are for. When a person lies, the theory goes, their heart will beat faster. Holding Randy's wrist and taking his pulse should let JB do the same thing as the machine. He could monitor Randy's heartbeats. At least that was the basic concept, JB had never actually done it, but here was an oppertunity to test it that he couldn't pass up.

JB took hold of Randy's wrist and found the pulse. It was there beating strong and steady. JB decided to ask a trick question that would cause Randy to lie, to test the idea out. If it didn't work JB could let go of the wrist and rely on what tics he could see to tell if Randy was being untruthful. Any gun in the arsenal was useful if it's applied right. "So, Randy, first question. Are you in jail?"

"Jeez, what a stupid..."

"Answer him, Randy." George stepped forward.

"Okay. Okay."

"A simple yes or no is all I'm asking for Randy." JB concentrated on the beats he felt under his fingers.

"All right. No, I'm not." And he smirked.

"Then your lying. You are phyisically currently in jail."

"Then yes."

"You're still lying. You haven't been charged with anything. You aren't serving a sentence."

Randy's pulse had now sped up. I'll be damned, JB was thinking, it works. As rapid as the pulse was, or as steady as it would get, it would give JB a sense of Randy's reaction to a given question. An idea if he was being truthful or not.

"Hey, then there's no way I can answer you. What gives?"

"I'm asking the questions, Randy. Second one. Were you Officer Barkley's informer? Yes or no?"

"Yes." Steady pulse.

"Were you paid for your services?"

"Yes." Faster beat.

"How were you paid? Did he give you money?"

"Yes." Even faster.

"Or maybe some other kind of payment?"

"No." Even faster.

"Come on, the truth." JB had caught him in a lie. JB could see it on his face. Randy was beginning to believe in what JB was doing.

"Okay. I did it so he wouldn't arrest someone." The pulse slowed.

"That's better. Who?"

"My sister."

"Who's that?"

"Molly. Molly Sharp."

"The hooker? The hooker is your sister?" Now that he had said it JB did notice a resemblance.

"Yeah. So what? She needed protection, so she wouldn't get hassled by Barkley or any of the other cops. If I finked for him he'd leave her alone. So I did it." His pulse was steady.

"Is that why you joined the drug dealing gang."

"Sure. Why else. I don't do that shit." Still steady.

"So Barkley got you inside so you could report when they had big buys happening?"

"That's right." Still steady. "But some money went missing and they blamed me. I was in trouble. So Barkley put me here to save my ass. It stinks, but its better than what that gang would do to me if I was outside." Faster pulse, but JB wasn't HOME sure if that was because of fear of reprisal from the gang or a lie.

"Money went missing, huh? How much money?"

"A lot. About eighty thousand."

Wow. And you got away with that much?"

"Naw. They had it all wrong. I didn't take shit." His

pulse sped up some, but JB didn't need his pulse to tell he wasn't being truthful. He could see it in Randy's face. By now JB had clicked to his tell. He blinked repeatedly when he was lying. Fast. So the guy was a thief. Was he a murderer too?

"What about Howard Fellows?" There was a faster beat to Randy's heart. "You implicated him in that drug case. Why did you do that?"

"Cause he was in it. Up to his neck. He was a front man for the gang. He made them look legit." His pulse was pounding to beat the band. There was even a Salsa rhythm.

"Come on, Randy. I knew Howard. He wasn't into drugs. What's the real reason?"

"All right." By now Randy was a true believer in what JB could do. He was thinking JB was some kind of mind reader. JB could really tell when he was lying. The truth was all that would set him free. "It was Barkley. He wanted Fellows out of the way. So did I. Fellows had found out about the drug thing. He wanted me to do the same thing Barkley had me doing. To rat on the gang. So, when Barkley wanted him out of the way it worked fine for me too...I went along with it. I lied about Fellows. I told the Chief that he was a member of the gang so he'd be put here in jail." The heartbeat slowed some.

"Why did Barkley want him in here?"

"How the hell should I know?" The pulse speeded up again. What was he lying about now? "Barkley said he wanted him gone. Since I wanted the same thing I didn't ask and Barkley didn't tell me his reasons. He just said what he wanted." This time Randy's pulse was steady at that fast speed.

"What about the day Howard Fellows was killed?" What do you know about that?" The pulse started pounding harder. If it kept up the guy was going to really have a stroke.

"He was in the library all day. Nobody saw him until the next morning when he was found hanging in there." JB noticed another increase in his pulse. And Randy was sweating. A bead of water poured down the side of his face.

"What about the cop that was on duty? Rickman?"

He heard Randy take a breath. To steady himself? JB felt the pulse start to slow.

"He was there. Doing his usual thing. Making our lives hell. What a jerk."

"Was there any sign that he was after Fellows?"

"Naw. Not more than anybody else. All the cops were harassing the guy some. He was supposed to have killed

Barkley. One of theirs. You shouldn't kill cops." The pulse was going again. Faster than normal. And his eyes were blinking like semaphore code. JB figured that Randy wasn't telling everything he knew. "Why are you asking?" he said. "You think Rickman might have done your friend in?" His pulse started to slow.

"Only asking questions, Randy. Pursuing possibilities."

"Well, I don't know nothing more." That set the pulse off fast again. He pulled his arm away. "I'm done." He stood.

"All right. But I may have more questions later."

"I'm not doing this no more. You're a fucking weirdo. Keep away from me." He turned and headed for the door. He ran up against George who was standing cliff like in the doorway.

"Move it" Randy raised his arm to strike.

George raised his club. It flashed a shiny black from the light. "You want this upside your head?"

"Wouldn't stop me, asshole."

"Maybe not. But there'd be a dent cross your skull that would slow you down."

Randy glared at George. George stood his ground and stared back. Randy considered his options then said, "Right." George nodded and stepped aside. Randy left the room.

George said, "It's like a high school recess yard around here. Who's got the biggest balls."

JB scoffed, "What are you? Westminster Cathedral?"

"I said balls, not bells."

"Well, they both clang don't they?"

George laughed then went after Randy to put him back in his cell.

JB sat there a minute thinking about what he'd just heard and how he felt about it. He was sure Randy knew more than he was saying. And what about that money he'd mentioned? Did Randy steal it from the gang? If he did, maybe Howard had found out about it and was doing his blackmailing thing again? That could be why Randy wanted Howard out of the HOME way. JB still thought Randy was involved in Howard's killing. But Rickman was a prime suspect too. Vince Barkley seemed to have both Randy and Terry Rickman under his thumb. He could have made either of them do about anything he wanted. And Vince wanted Howard out of the way. That would have been because of the blackmail Howard was pulling on Vince about the gay sex club. JB realized he would have to finish

Howard's notes on that story. He was pretty sure they would tell all about Barkley's involvement in the whole sordid mess. And Vince Barkley couldn't afford to have that secret life of his exposed. JB wondered again if Barkley's notebook might have some information on the club too. He would have to go over to Mrs. Barkley's house the next day to see if she would give the books to him. They could help him figure all this out.

George came back into the room. "Did you get what you wanted, JB?"

"Actually, I've ended up with more questions than before. But Randy did clear Howard of the drug charges. That's a step in the right direction. Did you know that Barkley had forced Randy to implicate Howard?"

"No, not specifically that, but, you know, the whole force knew that Vince was dirty. He would do anything, and I mean anything, to get a conviction. Tamper with evidence, beat on people, bribe witnesses. You name it. So it isn't a surprise that he had Howard framed."

"Why doesn't the Chief know about this?"

"Hey, Vince was a scary guy. A real bully. But he was also a hell of a suck-up around those who had more power than he did. He had the Chief completely fooled. He'd have pounded anyone of us into the ground if we'd told the Chief what he was pulling."

"So, he managed to intimidate the entire force?" George nodded. "He must have been a real prince of a guy. Well, Vince is gone now, and the Chief needs to be brought up to date on his character. Take the tapes from these interrogations and make sure he gets them. Okay, George?"

"Sure. But don't you want to talk to him."

"Yeah, but I don't have enough yet. All I have are suspicions. If I catch up with him later maybe I'll have something more concrete than the guessing I've been doing so far."

"All right. I'll pass on the message."

"Thanks."

After curtain, Len was removing his make-up when Sneed knocked on the door. "Come in, come in," Len said.

"What did you want, my Captain?"

"I've been thinking about what you said the last time we talked, and I've decided you need to get yourself a fella. At least for overnight. So, now that the show is over you and I are going to have a quick supper and then go out. I'm going to get you laid."

Sneed grinned like a Halloween pumpkin and said, "Let me get changed. My dressing room is just upstairs."

"Right. Then we'll spread some of Tinkerbell's dust and see what magic we can accomplish." Len chuckled.

Sneed moaned, then left to get ready.

Len had an ulterior motive for taking Sneed under wing. Earlier, between scenes, he'd had a chance to speak with the Croc and find out what he was thinking about New Wendy's situation. The director, and by extension, the producers, felt that New Wendy had in only those few scenes played become a liability to the show. She couldn't help it but her voice made her stand out from rest of the ensemble. She didn't blend with the rest of the cast. Audiences are expected to become involved in the overall effect a show is presenting; to believe that the cast is a representation of that presented reality. If one person stands out for a reason other than they are supposed too then it destroys that illusion. New Wendy's cartoon voice was doing exactly that. It was pulling the audience away from the show the cast was trying to present. She was going to be replaced. By the time she was singing the first notes of her last song the Croc was already on the phone to the producers. They were, in turn, arranging for her replacement to join the company in Denver, the next stop on the tour. A perfect example of how show business can be ruthless and cut-throat. The producers called the second runner-up to the original Wendy from the New York auditions. And she was available. New Wendy was out.

Len then decided to explain some of what he suspected to the Croc so that he would go along and help with a little plot Len was starting to work out. Something to draw the sneaky saboteur out from their hiding place. Len didn't have all the steps yet, but he knew he needed to have one thing done to make any of it work out. He needed the newest Wendy, instead of taking over the part she'd been hired for, to go first into the chorus for a few days. That way, he said to the Croc, she could become familiar with the cast, and the set, and the rhythm of the show. And that's exactly what Len convinced the director would happen. Next, Len got himself invited along to the airport to pick the woman up when she arrived in Denver. That would give him a chance to pull her aside and ask her not to mention to anyone that she was New Wendy's replacement. With that piece in place Len would then have time to come up with the final details of his plan. And all by the time they were settled and playing in Colorado.

Len also, after due consideration, had finally written New Wendy's mother, along with all the featured players, off his list of suspects. He was now completely convinced that the culprit was one of the women of the ensemble. What he needed to do was figure out which one.

That was why Len had invited Sneed out that night. To get the part he played in the plot set in motion. Sneed wasn't aware of it but he was going to play his on-stage part off-stage as well. Sneed, as Hook's cabin boy, carried orders to the crew in the play. Now Len wanted him to carry some gossip to a few of the women of the company. Since he was a tattletale of the first rank Len didn't doubt he would be happy to oblige. Sneed's job would be to let the ensemble women know that New Wendy was going to be replaced. That, Len knew, would set their ambition antennas to wagging. Then Sneed would report back to him what their reactions to the news had been. If the subversive was indeed one of them their first response to the news could tell Len a great deal.

Len passed on the information to Sneed over their meal in one of the many gay restaurants in San Francisco. After they'd eaten, he got them a cab. He whisked Sneed off to a bar on the edge of the Castro named *The Cloud Nine*. It was the West Coast version of New York's *Toad Hall*. The Cloud was a supreme twink bar amongst twink bars. The cab pulled up to the curb. Sneed peered out the window with anticipatory glee, literally bouncing on the seat at the prospect.

"There you go, Sneed, my boy. The guys in that place will love that pretty little butt of yours." Len was positive that when Sneed walked into the place looking like the seventeen going on eighteen youth that he played every night in the show there would be people trampled in the rush for him.

Waiting in front of the bar was a line of young men from the entrance to the end of the block. All of them in their twenties. Each lived up to their reputations. Twinkling was much in evidence. Fairy dust had been spread like Tinkerbell was flying on speed. Len told Sneed to make sure he had his ID with him. Looking the way he did he was sure to be carded. He patted his backside and nodded.

"Then get on that line and prepare to fly to your own personal sexual Neverland."

"Aren't you coming?" he asked.

"Your kidding. The only way I could get laid in there is if I painted my penis to look like a hundred dollar bill. But you, my dear, will be a shining star. So go on, play Lost Boy to your hearts content tonight. But remember, there's an eight-thirty AM call at the train station tomorrow morning."

The cab took Len back to his hotel.

It only took JB a few moments to walk around the corner to Goldy's place from the police station. It was cool inside the bar, and a relief from the afternoon heat. The sun tended to pound down and bleach out the gravel and tarred streets of this little Kansas plains town.

The place wasn't crowded. There were only two men playing pool and Eddie Falco sitting in what appeared to be his regular spot at the corner of the bar. He walked over to sit next to him and signaled Goldy for a draft.

He placed it in front of him and said, "Good to see you, Mr. Bent."

"JB, please."

"Okay, JB." He smiled. Goldy did have a friendly kind of smile.It gave him a plesant look that pointed directily to his personality. He was a kind and jovial man. Also he was overweight and wore an extra large tropical printed shirt to cover his protruding paunch. His face was round with crinkled amused eyes, and to hide the double chins he wore a full bushy beard. It gave him the look of a furry cuddlesome animal, a live teddy bear. He was a chubby chasers dreamboat. Okay, a dreambarge. "Can I get you something to eat?"

JB looked at his watch. It was almost three. "You know, I haven't eaten yet. It sounds good. What've you got that isn't beer nuts or pretzels?"

"We have a pretty good pizza. It only takes a minute. Will that do?"

"Yeah. Sounds good. How about you, Eddie. You want to share one with me?"

"Sure. I'll go halves with you."

"There you are, Goldy. One pizza for the two of us."

"So," Eddie said. "How's the looking into Howard's death going?'"

"You know its turning out to be a lot more than that. I'll also have to figure out who killed Vince Barkley. And I need to look into that story Howard was writing, and a couple of other things. I'm looking at about four other things besides Howard being killed."

"It's enough to keep you busy then?" Goldy said as he set the frozen pizza in the toaster oven behind the bar.

"More than enough. The worst of it is I've only got a couple of pages done on my own book so far, and those corrections have to be done."

"What are you going to do next?" Eddie asked

"Well, tonight I have that poker game I was invited too. And tomorrow I want to go over to Mrs. Barkley's house again. I want to look at Vince's case notebooks. There might be some information in them that will help. And, as I said, I still have to go through Howard's notes. They're sitting in a drawer in my hotel room. And, I've got dinner with my Mother tomorrow night. So I'll be busy. By the way, Goldy, I was going to ask you. What's a good gay restaurant over in Wichita?" JB figured that if his mother wanted to be included in his life she may as well see it up close.

"Are you kidding? You're in the Bible Belt, JB. There isn't any such thing out here. There's only one bar in Wichita that could even be called gay friendly." He thought a moment. "I suppose there is one place you could eat. At least the waiters and the manager are all gay. And the bar is a kind of meeting place for Wichita's gay crowd. It's pissey though. A jacket is required."

"I guess it'll have to do. What's the name?"

"*La Maison de Butterfly.*"

JB raised his eyebrows. "Subtle." He would never get used to the codes that gays used to identify themselves to other gays. Friends of Dorothy and the like. Names of business' would indicate if they were open to gay patronage. A place called *The Gay Lantern,* or *The Cock Pit,* with the inevitable rooster as its logo, told you where your kind were welcome. It was all a part of that old time closeted underground thinking still prevelant outside a big city.

JB said. "Can I use your phone?"

Goldy reached under the bar and pulled out the instrument. JB pulled it close. "What's the number?"

It only took a few minutes for him to make a reservation for nine the next evening. By that time the pizza was done and sitting between Eddie and himself. JB hung up, then picked up a piece of the pie and began to eat.

Between bites of his own slice Eddie asked, "So, what's in that story of Howard's that's so important? I've heard it would shock the whole town to its core."

Goldy said, "I heard that too. The rumors are probably worse than the reality though. At least I would hope so. This town has enough to gossip going about already. We make *Dynasty's* doings look like croquet at Sunnybrook Farm."

"Hell, I don't know what all Howard wrote down," JB answered. "There might be names, or more information on Vince. It's a packet of notes and scraps of paper. Howard hadn't gotten around to writing the story yet."

"Really?" Eddie reached across JB for a jar of parmesan cheese."That's odd, because Howard always was so organized. He was always ahead of the game." As Eddie's head passed him JB noticed a few dark flakes behind his ear. Mother had always said to wash behind your ears. Eddie obviously hadn't been told the same by his. JB looked closer. It was paint. Black paint. Eddie must be doing some home improvement projects. Or maybe he'd been visiting Molly. "So you and Howard stayed friends did you, Eddie?"

"Uh...No, not really. We saw each other around town, but we weren't great buddies."

"How are Vince's notes going to help?" Goldy asked.

JB took his attention off Eddie and looked at him. "Same thing," he said. "I figure these things out by piecing together all the bits of information I gather. It's like a big patchwork quilt that ends up covering the person responsible. For instance, me going to this poker game tonight. I don't really enjoy playing poker, but if I can get some little piece that might help it will be worth it. It could solve the case."

"Well, watch out for Rickman," Goldy said. "He's not one to mess around with."

"Goldy, that's exactly what I'm going to find out."

"What?"

"If Rickman can be messed around with. Howard was writing about a gay cop club. Rickman is a cop, and even you said that the Poker Guys are a little boys club. I need to find out if the games they play are maybe more adult. Triple X even."

They sat at the bar, Eddie and JB, the rest of the afternoon talking. JB found out more about how the town had changed since he'd left it all those years ago. It had gotten larger, of course, there was even a new tract of houses out on Porter Road that were called suburbs. Laughingly, JB was sure. And there was a new high school, all low glass fronted buildings and modern architecture, with a full football field. There was a canning plant now over on the east side of town. It gave needed jobs to the locals. And the town council was discussing letting a private prison open over on the north side. That too would supply jobs. There was even talk that a *K-Mart* would be opening soon. Peebels was being dragged into the late 20th century whether it wanted to or not.

Terry Rickman arrived, still in uniform, at about five-thirty. He explained he was just off his shift for his days off. That was how he could play in the game that evening. Normally he would have been on night duty at the jail. He had a varied slate of jobs to do with the Peebels police force. One night on patrol, one night as jail house guard, then a day shift.

Terry joined them for another beer and then took JB in his car to the place where they would play their poker game. He drove out to Porter Road and into the new Rolling Hills housing development Eddie had mentioned. This was the plains, the only hills JB knew of around there were the speed bumps built into the streets.

The roadways were tar paved and seemed to lead out into the middle of empty fields on all the side streets. The streets themselves only had one or two houses on each side facing each other and were blank lots with construction supplies piled on them the rest of the way. There were names like Enchanted Valley Road and Mystic Elm Way. The only trees visible were scrawny, limp leafed, and new. They all seemed desperate for a drink of water.

The houses were all built to the same plans. It looked like there were only three variations, mostly in the placement of the front door and the garage. The entire development couldn't have been more than a year old with dirt yards and under-grown flowerbeds the predominate landscaping. They stopped in front of a white and blue trimmed ranch and parked. JB followed Rickman up the flagstone pathway to the front and waited while he rang the bell.

It was opened by the guy that worked in the station as the dispatcher/general clerk/computer operator. His name was Jess Havers. He was young, in his mid-twenties, blond, and cute. In your mid-twenties you could still be called cute and get away with it.

Sitting on the living room couch was another cop. Although he was wearing civilian clothes JB could still tell he was a cop from the buzz of his haircut to the clunky heavy soled black shoes he wore. His name was Cleat Durning, and it turned out he was with the Kansas State Patrol. When the Chief had a particularly serious case he would call on them to help.

The three men stood in a group and held each other's hands. Then there was a football huddle grunt and some ritual fist tapping and rubbing between the men. Goldy had said they had secret handshakes and the like. It all looked like the kind of things that little boys who wouldn't let stinky girls into their clubs used to do. Then Terry pulled JB into the middle of the circle. He stood there, feeling ridiculous, while they shifted around until they had circled him two times. Then they all held out their fists and he was expected to slap each of them with his own. Male posturing. Silly stuff, to say the least.

JB hit the fists all around and was given a beer. The circle broke and they stood looking at each other like teenagers at a junior high school dance. Terry said, "Is this all that's gonna be here tonight?" Looking over at JB he added, "We usually have about eight or ten for one of these games."

Jess said, "Yeah, but since Vince died a few have decided to lay low for awhile. They'll be back. Give them a little time."

"Shit, it means lower pots. And fewer choices."

"Well, you've got that covered already."

"We'll see. I'm not so sure."

This cryptic talk between Terry and Jess caused JB's radar to start beeping. What were they talking about? He wasn't sure? Choices? What did that mean? He decided to keep quiet at this point. Maybe they would say more as they went along that he could understand.

"Well," Cleat said. "If this is it for tonight then let's play. I don't think it's so bad at that. Let's get started."

"Sure," Jess said. "In the dining room."

They walked into the room. The dining table was laid out with cards, chips, and coasters.

"Use the coasters. Okay? Evie will have a shit-fit if there are stains on her table."

"Where is she?"

"I sent her over to her mothers for the night. And she took the kid, so we have the place to ourselves."

"That's what we need. Now, let's see who wins tonight." Terry rubbed his hands together.

They sat and the cards were dealt for a game of five card draw. JB wasn't sure if he should win or lose, not knowing the consequences of either result. Since he didn't play poker all that often it didn't matter that much. He would probably lose anyway.

They played three or four hands and there was the regular man-shit bull-con back and forth between all of them. Lousy cards, complaints about work and the boss, not enough money in the pot. The usual. After one hand Jess threw down his cards and said, "Damn, I'm on bottom again. That's the third time in the last two months."

"Ah, shut the hell up," Terry said. "You know you love it, so quit your bitching."

Now what did that mean? JB wondered. If one of his gay friends back in New York had said it JB would know immediately he was going to be the passive partner for sex. Out here in the parochial plains it might be something entirely different. Or was it?

They continued playing, and five or six hands later, Cleat said, "That's it, partner. We can stop playing right now. I get what I want." He stood up and stretched. "I'm getting another beer. You want one, Jess?"

"Sure, I'll come with you." He got up and the two went off into the kitchen. JB put down his cards. "Well, Terry, it doesn't look like I'm going to win big tonight. I'm losing here. Where's the bathroom?"

Terry directed him down the hall. As he passed through the hall he passed another doorway into the kitchen. In there, standing next to the icebox, JB saw Cleat and Jess in an embrace, just finishing a kiss.

Gay Cop Club! Hello. It looked like Jess was certainly going to be screwed tonight. And in the biblical sense at that. JB didn't need a brick upside his head to figure some things out. He went to the john, peed, and headed back to the living room.

Jess and Cleat were no longer by the icebox when JB passed the kitchen door this time. They had probably retired to the bedroom. Terry wasn't sitting at the table anymore either. He had moved to the couch and had turned on the TV. "Come on over, JB. Look at this."

He went over. The TV was running a porn tape on the VCR. A humungous breasted woman was merrily humping a not very attractive man with a very large dick. All that bouncing flesh looked absolutely ludicrous.

"Good God," JB said. "No wonder some women are so angry all the time. If I had those things bouncing on my chest every day I'd be pissed off too."

Terry looked at JB with a wondering expression. "You don't think that's hot?"

"Why would I? Christ, the guy's a total dog. You know there is better porn than this available. You only need to spend more than two-ninety-eight for it."

Terry rubbed at his crouch. "I think it's hot."

"No accounting for taste."

"Come on, JB, let's get it on. Give me a blowjob, huh?"

"Not on your life, Terry." JB sat on the armrest of the couch. "For one thing I don't find you particularly attractive. You just aren't my type."

"But, you're a fag. Aren't blowjobs and stuff what you guys do? Come on, do me."

"Terry, would you go down on just any woman that offers? Even if they're the biggest skank for three counties?" He shook his head. "I thought so. Well, we gay men are exactly the same. We have our likes and dislikes the same as you so-called straight folk. Some of us even have real taste." Terry stopped rubbing himself. "And, furthermore, you're a married man. That fact alone would stop me. I make it a strict rule that I don't get between two people that are connected. By marriage or in an affair. I think love and relationships are way too hard to find in this wacked out world without some third party messing them up. I don't get involved with married men. Gay or straight. I simply don't do adultery."

"It isn't."

"Why? Because it's with a guy and not a woman. You really

think that it isn't cheating on your wife? You need a reality check, Terry. Cheating is cheating. No matter the gender. No matter how you rationalize it. You know what? I think you'd better take me back to my hotel now. This night is over."

The game had accomplished one of JB's goals anyway. He had found the club that Howard had been investigating. It turned out that it was just sad. JB didn't think Howard would have won any prizes exposing it. And he probably would have broken up quite a few relationships in town once the publication of the article hit the fan.

In the car back to town, Terry tried again to seduce JB into doing something with him, and again JB turned him down. "Let me make this clear, Terry. I am not interested in having sex with you under any circumstances. What I came to this poker game for was to check out some information I had on this club of yours. Howard's notes would probably have been enough, but I had to see for myself."

"Howard's notes? For what?"

"For his story. You knew about that, right?"

"No. I didn't know anything about a story. But I'll bet that's why Vince had Howard arrested. To stop any story Howard might have been writing."

"Correct. At least that's what I think happened. I want to check his notebook to confirm it."

"His book? Why do you want that?"

"I think it has his notes on the whole sordid mess in it. All you cops keep notes on every detail of a case. Even ones that are dirty. Didn't Vince keep a notebook?"

"Yeah. But I saw it once. It was gibberish. He wrote in code."

"Well, I like puzzles. Maybe I can break his code. I'll find out tomorrow when I get it from his wife."

"Rose?"

"Yeah. Vince's effects were sent to her. I'm going to talk to her tomorrow. By the way, Terry, you were on duty the night that Howard died, right?" He nodded. "Why didn't you make him go to his cell when the jail locked down for the night?"

"Because he wanted to keep reading. I asked him right before lights out. He said he wanted to stay. When the jail shut down for the night he couldn't see well enough to read, so he stayed in there where he had enough light."

"Is that policy?"

"No, I should have made him go back to his cell, but I cut

him some slack. I had no idea that he was going to do what he did. Who could know?"

Terry left JB off in front of the hotel and drove off. JB shook his head. What a sorry life Terry must lead. And his poor wife. Terry's operating theory was what she didn't know wouldn't jeopardize what he needed from his marriage. That was a cover. His marriage was a convenience that he could hide behind and not be thought gay. So he lied and equivocated and excused and totally ignored any of the moral implications of his actions. JB was quite sure that Terry sat in his church every Sunday and felt no guilt at all for what he was doing. That was screwed up thinking in his estimation. JB didn't get how Terry could sleep with another person and not think it was wronging his life partner. And it didn't matter what gender the partner was, man or woman. You sleep with someone else and you're cheating. Simple. Clear. No equivocation.

The hotel lobby was empty as JB walked across it. The elevator slid up the two stories to the third floor and he went to his room. When the key opened the door he immediately sensed that something wasn't right. What was going on?

He turned on the lights and looked around. When he looked at the desk what was wrong was right there in front of him. His galleys were missing. The original manuscript was still there. All three hundred thirty-seven pages of it were piled up next to the empty spot where he had left the galleys he needed to correct that morning. What the hell?

He called downstairs and asked who had been in his room. JB knew he had locked the door when he left so someone had to have come in. The night clerk wasn't much help. He hadn't started his shift until eight and there had been nobody since then that had even inquired after JB.

He would have to wait until the next day to question anyone about the disappearance. What the heck? Why the galleys and not the manuscript? And what about his deadline? He knew he could get another copy of the galleys when he got back to New York, but it would put him way late for the delivery to the printers. Well, this was a fine mess.

JB knew he had to get up first thing the next day so he went in and showered. That way he could get downstairs early the next morning. Then he pulled out Howard's notes and started to look through them. He skimmed them looking for names and dates, any indication that Howard might have had that someone meant him harm.

He found it on a piece of yellow blue lined scratch paper. It detailed Randy Sharp's theft of the money from that gang of drug dealers he was involved with. Howard had discovered the double-double cross on Randy's part by overhearing the right conversation—not only was Randy ratting out the gang to Barkley, but he was also skimming large amounts of money from the gang. When the gang leader found out about it he put a hit out on Randy. That was standard operating procedure for gangs. You take you die. That was what got Randy into protective custody at the Peebels City jail.

Howard had been looking into the drug trade in town. To do that he had hung around the biker bar the dealers frequented. He called it undercover work, but JB suspected that Howard really liked the rough trade that hung out there. One night he'd overheard the gang leader bragging that he was going to kill Randy for stealing. It gave Howard his great idea. Howard must have seen that money Randy took as his way out. It was drug money. That meant it was free money, loose bills with no way to trace them. It could get Howard out of Peebels and over to Wichita. JB suspected that when he met Randy in the jail after his arrest he fell back on his blackmailing tricks and went after him. That's what Howard was talking about when he gave JB that key at the jail. How Howard had actually got the key JB didn't know. Probably stole it from Randy's cell. The cells were left open all day, right? So JB had the key in his pocket all along.

That meant Randy had been telling some of the truth when JB questioned him. What had Howard threatened Randy with? Exposure? Something concerning his sister Molly? And how had Randy reacted? Was he the one that had killed Howard? Was it that anger JB had seen just under the surface when he questioned him? Or was Howard being killed part of a plan Vince had instigated? Could it have been Terry that did it? Both Terry and Randy had access to Howard that night. Either of them could have done it. JB fell asleep before he could read the rest of the notes to find out how Vince and Terry and Randy and gang leaders and drugs were all tied into this very messy set of crimes.

He woke up at six the next morning and found Howard's notes spread and crumpled all over the bed. He must have slept very fretfully to have made such a mess. He didn't feel at all rested and was sure another couple of hours of sleep would have been helpful. Instead, he rubbed at his itching eyes, gathered the notes, and put them back in their envelope. Then stashed them back in the desk drawer.

He quickly got dressed and went downstairs. The day clerk was now on and JB questioned him about somebody being in his room. He wasn't any help since he was only a relief day clerk. The regular day man was on his days off and this guy was only part-time. Of no help. JB asked about the maids. The same thing, a different crew today than yesterday. He couldn't catch a break. JB left a report of the stolen galleys at the desk with instructions to give it to the manager.

JB went again across the alley and into the police station. At the desk he was told the Chief wasn't in yet, he was still at breakfast, so JB decided to wait. While he was sitting there he filled out a police report on his stolen galleys. About a half-hour after he started the Chief wandered in, a toothpick held in between his front teeth.

"JB," he said. "I was hoping you'd show up today. Come into my office." JB followed behind him down the hall and through his door. The Chief aimed right for his chair. JB sat in the other one. The Chief picked up his phone and asked whoever answered for a cup of coffee, then asked if JB wanted anything. JB hadn't had a shot of caffeine yet so he said, "Sure."

"It'll be here in a little bit," the Chief said as he hung up. "Now, I listened to your interview tapes from yesterday. What is it you think you got out of them? Other than telling a kid to get out of town, and showing sympathy toward a drunk there wasn't much that I could figure."

"What about Randy saying that he lied about Howard's involvement with the drug gang? That's something. It vindicates Howard and shows that he was telling the truth about being railroaded on false charges. Charges made up by Vince Barkley. And I gained a lot of insight into Vince's character too. What did you call him? One of your best officers? Best isn't the opinion of the majority of people I've talked to so far. Vince Barkley wasn't a good cop, Chief. He was corrupt, a bully, a tyrant, and as dirty as they come. He was capable of doing about any dishonest act you could think of. He was, in any vernacular, a bad cop, Chief Rotelli."

He squirmed in his seat. "Yeah, I don't like it, but I guess that's true. I did some checking of my own after I heard what was on the tape. I have to admit he did have me fooled. What are you going to do now?"

"I want to talk to Rose Barkley. I'm going over there this morning. I think those notebooks of his are important."

Then the deputy came in with a tray. Over their coffee the Chief and JB discussed a couple of other things. Things only peripherally involved with Howard's case. JB told him what he had discovered about the gay cop club but left out the names of the people involved, since he saw no reason to get them in trouble with their boss. Jobs could still be lost in Kansas for even a suspicion of being gay. There was nothing in place that gave gay men or women any job security, housing protections, or any of the basic human rights that most people take for granted. That's the horrible gay agenda that the religious right always talks about. Gay people only want the same basic respect and protections that all Americans have. How insidious can that be? The Chief and JB also discussed the disappearance of his galleys. JB told him he had written a report and handed it over to the clerk out front. The Chief said he would look into it.

When they finished JB headed for the hotel parking lot. He got into his borrowed cab and headed over to see Vince Barkley's widow, Rose, one more time.

While Sneed was getting his biological urges soothed the crew of *Hook and Wendy* was packing up the sets and getting them moved by truck from the theater to the train station. All of it, the pirate ship, the Countess' ballroom, even the Indian village fit into one freight car and were ready the next morning to be transported to the next city they were to play—Denver, Colorado.

The cast was gathered at the station at eight-thirty the next morning and was on the way by nine. They would be ensconced at the Brown Hotel by early evening, and rehearsing for a two week run on their new stage by ten the next day.

Len spent the first part of the train trip in the Croc's compartment looking over the pictures and resumes of the women in the chorus. He was trying to figure out which one of them might be his saboteur. He was able to immediately eliminate any of the women under Wendy's seventeen. They would be too young to play Wendy so would have no motive. That left him with seven people. He cut out two of them because they were altos. Wendy's part called for a soprano so they wouldn't be considered. Wendy's part called for a soprano. Another two were cut because of weight and height. One woman played a comic Indian squaw in her scenes—and the other woman was the understudy for the younger, shorter children. Neither of them would be cast in Wendy's part, so, once again, there was no motive.

That left Len with three suspects. Those three would be the actors he would want to watch. They were the one's he had intended Sneed to gossip with, and they were the one's whose reaction to New Wendy losing her part in the show Len was most interested in knowing about. He went looking for Sneed.

Len found him curled up in his seat in the passenger car sound asleep. But with a smile on his face. Len sat down opposite him and coughed. Sneed stirred but didn't wake. Another couple of coughs from Len finally got his eyes to open. He sat up and stretched out his arms. "Hello, Captain. I must have slept like the dead."

"Or the satisfied?"

"Oh my, yes. Delightfully. Thank you."

"So you enjoyed the bar then?"

"You know I didn't get in. I met someone on line and we decided to go from there."

"Speedy little fucker, aren't you?"

"That's what Andrew said last night."

"Listen, did you get a chance to talk to the girls in the company?"

"Sure. I did that too. At that ungodly hour we got up this morning. It was still dark, for God's sake. I was exhausted."

"That's what comes from spreading fairy dust all over creation, or all over Andrew, you sissy Mary, So, tell me, what were the women's reactions?."

"They were excited, I guess. And full of questions. When was it going to happen? Who would replace her?"

"From all three of them?"

"Which three?"

"Oh, I was looking at Nancy, Marta, and Gwen."

"Not Gwen. She didn't seem to care much. She only said 'poor girl' about her."

"Okay, Sneed. Thanks."

"No, thank you. Say do you know any places in Denver?"

"I might. But you should be able to sniff them out all by yourself from now on. Once a boy queen's gaydar is engaged it can't be turned off. From now on another fairy in your vicinity will come in loud and queer."

Len went to the dining car for lunch, and in the space of time it took him to go from his soup to his sandwich two of the three chorus women he suspected came to his table to pry information out of him. Neither of them were very subtle in their approach either. Nancy tried being cute and Marta used a blunter approach by just asking outright. Both of them wanted to know how the director was going to replace New Wendy. Were they having auditions? Picking one or the other? Or throwing darts at a list of their names? Len admitted to not having a clue. And he didn't. How could he? He hadn't worked out all the details himself yet. So he wasn't lying to them. But he did withhold what little information he did have simply because he wanted to prolong the guessing game so he could gauge the women's degree of desire. How far would they go to get the part?

As Len was ready to finally take a bite from his chicken salad sandwich New Wendy's mother showed up. She was not a contented woman. She stood over his table like the Wicked Witch of the West. Where was a falling house when you needed one?

"What kind of guff are you handing my daughter," she shrilled. Margaret Hamilton couldn't have done it better.

"Excuse me? To what are you referring?" An attitude such as hers could cause Len to return one in kind

"You've been telling my daughter that she doesn't have to pay attention to what I tell her. How dare you undermine my rights as a parent."

"I beg your pardon. I only told the girl that when she was eighteen she could make her own decisions. I do think that's the way it still works. You turn eighteen and you get to be your own person. You get to vote and everything."

"Well, that won't happen. She won't be eighteen for ages."

"You're wrong there. She's seventeen now. Or so you said when she signed her contract. She is, isn't she?"

"Of course she is."

"Then you have until her next birthday. After that she's on her own. Now run along. I'd like to eat."

The woman sniffed, then turned and left.

That cinched it. Len was making that phone call. The one to Shelbyville, Indiana. Especially after that little display. He would do it as soon as he was in his room in Denver.

Notes From Home

W hen JB got to the street where Rose Barkley lived he ended up having to park a couple of blocks away from the house. Her block was packed full of cars sitting bumper to bumper on both sides of the street. As JB drove by her place he saw a couple of kids playing out on the lawn and several men standing on the porch smoking and talking.

JB walked back to the house and went up her walkway. He passed the gathering of men, who eyed him suspiciously, and went into the house. It looked like he had arrived while Vince's wake was in progress. JB hadn't realized he had been buried that morning.

It was a weird phenomenon in the Midwest that funerals tended to take on a muffled sort of festive air. It was the only time many of these people saw each other from year to year. A gathering of the clan, for whatever purpose, was occasion for catching up on what was going on in their lives. So there was laughter and gossip and news to be passed around. There was food galore, kids running and playing, men gathered in bunches to partake of sips from the bottles surreptitiously hidden in suit coats and back pockets.

Rose, dressed in a short sleeved black crepe dress, sat on a slipper chair in a back corner of the living room. She was surrounded by several women who acted as a protective guard around her. Rose would look up at the people who came up to her and speak with them in a sorrowful soft voice. She held a crumpled handkerchief in her hand that she dabbed at her eye on occasion. Odd, considering she had showed little remorse over her husband's death only the day before. JB supposed she felt she was required to fulfill the other mourner's expectations, regardless of how she really felt herself.

He went across the room and waited while a portly gentleman leaned over and spoke with her. When he moved on JB stepped up.

She looked up at him and said, "Mr. Bent. Thank you for coming." She dabbed at the corner of her eye. What an actress. Except she couldn't squeeze a tear. A single tear running down her cheek would have made it perfect.

"I'm sorry to disturb you at this most regrettable time, Mrs. Barkley, but I came for a favor." JB could play the game with the best of them.

"Favor?"

"Yes. The Chief informed me that he had sent over your husband's effects from the station. I was wondering if I could look at them? Would it be too much trouble?"

"My, no, of course not." She stood. "I have them in the other room. Come on, I'll take you." One of her women friends offered to do it for her. "No. No. I'll be fine. Follow me, Mr. Bent." She headed off across and around the other guests to a set of dark wood sliding doors on the other side of the room. She slid them open and stood aside. JB walked past her and into what was probably Vince Barkley's office. On the library table under the window was a cardboard box. Rose indicated that JB could look in it as she slid the heavy wooden doors shut.

"I really appreciate this. I'm sorry I'm taking you away from your company."

"Not at all. I needed a break from them anyway. Nice people, but far too solicitous. It gets on my nerves." She sat in the wooden swivel chair at the desk, then reached into her skirt pocket and pulled out a pack of cigarettes. She lit one, and picked at her lip to remove the piece of tobacco that was always left behind. She blew out the smoke she had inhaled, and said, "I should be ashamed of myself. I quit these things years ago. But all this has got me started again. Well, Mr. Bent, did you find out my husband was a degenerate and a pervert as I told you?"

"I did find out he wasn't a very nice person. He was

involved in some pretty shady dealings."

"As I suspected. I don't know what any of you expect to find in that box, Mr. Bent. He didn't keep much at the station."

"Oh, I was looking for his notebooks. All cops keep them for the cases they're working on. Your husband had my friend Howard falsely arrested for his involvement in a drug case he was investigating. I wanted to see what he had to say about it."

"Well, there are notebooks in that box. But they've already been gone through."

"Already? By who, Mrs. Barkley"?

"One of his fellow officers was here earlier. He said he was taking over Vince's cases and wanted to use his notes. I don't see how they would help. Vince, like all dishonest people, didn't trust anyone. He wrote his notes in a code he made up. So it all looked like a bunch of jumbles out of the Sunday papers."

"Who was that, Mrs. Barkley? Who went through this box?"

"Oh, I have no idea who it was. Just another officer on the Peebels police force. He brought his wife and then asked to go through the box. I know I should have known who Vince worked with, but I didn't. I never met most of the people that knew Vince, and I didn't care too. I'm sure they were all heathens and immoral characters anyway."

JB picked up the black notebooks out of the box. There were three. Inside the covers there were dates that the contents covered. The last one he found was dated up to three months before, and each book seemed to cover anywhere from six to nine months each. Inside the books was page after page of what looked like random letters, one after another, not spelling any recognizable words. The code that Vince used to hide his jottings. The dates, which weren't in a code, indicated there should have been another book that wasn't finished and covered the last few months up to his death. It wasn't in the box.

"Is it possible that the man that looked in here could have taken the last book that Vince was working on?"

"I suppose. I didn't watch him while he went through the thing. You should ask his wife. She's still here. She's with the church auxiliary ladies. They generously came over to help while all this was going on. I don't know her well, but it is a lovely gesture on their part. She's helping out in the kitchen. Would you like me to get her for you? It won't take a minute."

"Could you. That would be such a help."

Mrs. Barkley stood, crushed out her cigarette, and left the room to get the cop's wife. JB leaned over the table and opened the window behind the lace curtains. Then waved at the smoke to get it moving toward the outside. He had quit smoking a couple of years before, and swore then he wouldn't be one of those people that wave their arms around at other smokers. Well, here it was some time later and his arms were waving like a cheerleader at a football rally. The rancid smell of the burned tobacco alone made him nauseous.

While JB waited he took a look at the notes Vince had made in his notebooks. Each page was started with a number. Seven on one, twelve on another, three on the page after that. Then on the next line down were written letters. Sequenced as if they were words but only letters strung together, not spelling anything.

Like this:

3

Vxvshfw iq fxvwrqb rq srfhvvlrq fkj.

Another page had:

6

Muotm zu otzkxbokc qtuct jxam jkgrkx Puk X.

JB figured it was probably a simple switch code, one letter for another, but he would need some time to figure it out. First he knew he would have to find the repeated words like "it", "the", or "but". Once he had that he could figure out what letters Vince was substituting for the correct letters. Then he could figure the rest of the code and translate the notes back into proper English.

The office doors slid open and JB looked up.

He was, to say the least, surprised and delighted by the sight of the woman standing in the doorway. And she was a woman now, not the girl he had known before he left Peebels twenty years before. She looked a little older, but didn't they all, and she was maybe a couple of pounds heavier, but weren't they all. There were a few lines at the corners of her eyes, and the folds beside her mouth were a bit deeper—and so were JB's, thank you. She was, however, still as breathtaking as she had been in high school.

The lady was Kathy Miller. Kathy was JB's old girlfriend and best of all companion from school. She had been his beloved beard all the way from junior high school on up. She was the girl everyone thought JB was going to marry. They were thought of as the perfect match, and dated every weekend. They went to all the event's school kids were prone too. Rallies, dances, and the like. They were even voted cutest couple at their tenth grade cotillion. She was also the first person, after JB finally figured it out for himself, to know he was gay, the first to not care if he was, and his confidant and friend forever.

"My God, Kathy. I was hoping I would run into you while I was in town."

Her hand went to her mouth. "Oh, JB, I can't believe it. Mrs. Barkley said there was someone who wanted to talk to me about my husband. I didn't guess it would be you."

They came together in a quick embrace. And in a voice coming from JB's shoulder, she said. "How good you look. You've become quite polished in the last twenty years."

He held her at arm's length. "And you're as lovely as I ever thought you were. You look terrific."

She fussed with her hair. "You always were a big fat liar. I look frumpy. I know I do."

"Not in the least. You look the same as when we went to the prom."

"Now you've gone too far. I might have believed you up until then. JB, I'm forty. I look forty. However, you might get away with thirty something if I didn't know better."

"Why don't we both admit we've held up pretty well, and go on from there?" JB smiled. "Now, come on and sit. I have a hundred questions to ask."

They sat facing each other and started talking.

A half-hour later JB had found out that she was still living there in Peebels, had married once before and divorced, had a child from that marriage, a little girl now twelve, and was active in the church, the PTA, and took pottery classes on Tuesday nights. She had married her current husband only a few years before. It was a story told a thousand times by women her age all over the country. She had achieved what most every young Kansas girl graduating in 1963 wanted from her life. Women's liberation hadn't made many inroads into Kansas way back then. JB hoped she was happy. And he had good reason to be wondering about that.

JB found out that her new husband was none other than Terry Rickman. That Terry Rickman. The cop who had gone through Vince's box and taken the last notebook. The cop who JB was beginning to believe was a prime suspect in Howard's death. And the cop who had tried to have sex with him the night before. A charter member of the notorious Peebels gay cop sex club Howard had been planning to expose.

JB wasn't even that surprised at a married man looking for gay sex. That happened way too often. Everywhere. Even in New York, where being gay was mostly acceptable. There were even rumors that Malcolm Forbes, married millionaire publisher, seen dating Elizabeth Taylor after a very public divorce, would proposition his male interns. So the phenomena ran through all strata of society. What bothered JB was that the straying husband in this case was married to a friend of his, and she obviously had no clue as to her husband's extracurricular activities. That was both sad and, JB was thinking, really tacky. It was also the main reason he was trying to figure out if her marriage was a happy one or not.

Because the information JB processed caused him to face a real dilemma. Should he tell Kathy what her husband was up to? Or leave it alone? There were more than the usual ramifications to this knowledge about Terry. It wasn't simply that he was cheating on his wife—that was something that too many wives had to face. Each of them had to decide if they were willing to forgive their guy or not. But, in this case, there were health issues to think about too. There was AIDS to consider. Was it possible Terry was infected? He had sex with men. Was Terry being safe? JB wasn't so sure. He hadn't seen any evidence that he was, but they hadn't gotten that far into it for the subject to come up the night before. However, what about the others Terry was sleeping with? Was he safe with them?

AIDS was devastating JB's community back home. There were more than twenty-thousand deaths due to AIDS reported by the CDC since 1981. And the disease was steadily moving all across the country, and, that meant, inevitably into the straight community too. And JB didn't think Terry would be able to convince Kathy that he was suddenly a hemophiliac. JB hated to be the one who would have to tell Kathy what was going on, but he felt there was no choice. Her daughter needed a mother, and Kathy didn't deserve what could be the consequences of her husband's actions.

"So, Kathy, I'm asking about your husband for a couple of reasons..."

She was, of course, completely flabbergasted by what JB was telling her. Who could blame her? She also had a more than expected reaction. She was pissed. Mad as hell. The rest of it, the sorrow, the sadness, would come later. JB was sure of that.

For the first few moments she was unbelieving, but with the knowledge that JB had no reason to lie, she quickly became accepting of what was happening in what she thought of as her perfect life. After that first shock, and her first tears, she went to her bag and pulled out a book. She held it out to JB. It was the notebook that Terry had taken from the cardboard box of Vince's belongings. "Terry gave it to me to keep before he left here to go to work. I don't want it, JB. You take it. Burn him with it if you can. I want that son of a bitch dead. Out of my life."

"Honey, I know you're angry. But, you need to think about this for awhile. Before you confront him. Anger isn't the best emotion to carry you through this."

"And what better? The bastard has put me at risk. He's practically made my daughter an orphan. I want him gone."

"Now, you don't know if you've been infected. There are tests to be taken. There's been a test available since last year. You can find out."

"Is there? I didn't know that. I'll check with my doctor. Right away." She grabbed her bag, pulled out an address book, went to the phone and made a call. Minutes later she hung up. "I have an appointment for this afternoon." In a small town you could still get an appointment with a doctor the same day. In New York it could take up to two weeks.

"Will you come with me, JB. I'm frightened."

"Of course, but you know it's going to take some time for you to find out the results. You have to decide what you want to do now."

"Well, first, I have to make my excuses to the ladies in the kitchen, then we'll go to my appointment. Okay?"

"Fine."

Notes From The Road

The train pulled in to Denver and the cast dispersed in every direction, all with instructions to meet at the theater the next morning at ten. There was important information that had to be announced and all of them should be there. Len already knew what information it was. The Croc had worked it out with him during the rest of the train ride into town. However, there were still a couple of things Len needed to accomplish before the next morning.

It was still early in the afternoon so that left him the rest of the day and that night for getting ducks gathered and in nice neat rows. Right that moment, however, he only had a little more than an hour before he was to meet with the director and travel out to the airport. He grabbed a cab and told the driver to go to the Brown Hotel in downtown Denver. That took thirty minutes. It was another twenty minutes before he was in his room and could make his phone call. In Indiana it was already late afternoon and he wanted to call there before the offices closed for the day. He dialed and waited.

The clerk picked up after three rings and sounded as if she had been trying to leave her office. Len started out with an apology for the late hour of his call and then explained what he was looking for. Would she be able to search the records and find out the birth date of a city resident from the name only?

The woman was a friendly type and said that it wouldn't be a problem. Then added that their office had recently switched all the records over to a computer, and the darn things made it so easy. She took the name and put him on hold.

He waited. The laminated card with the hotel amenities took up the time, along with the Muzak playing on the phone. An orchestral arrangement of *Yummy, Yummy, Yummy, I Got Love In My Tummy* left Len shaking his head. The lady finally came back on the line with the information she had found. "Let's see, she was born here in 1973. October. Is that what you needed?"

"Yes. Exactly what I wanted. Could you send me a fax of that record?"

"Sure. Let me get paper...All right. The name and number?"

"That's Len Matthews. Care of the Brown Hotel, Denver Colorado..."

"Not *the* Len Matthews? The actor?"

"Well, that is my name and my profession. Is there something wrong?"

"Are you kidding? I'm a huge fan. I used to leave work early to watch you everyday on the TV. I loved *Regency Nights*. Oh, my God, Len Matthews. You were my favorite character."

"Well, thank you. That's nice to hear." It was. That people still remembered Len from the soap opera he had done was pleasing. As long as they didn't go nuts about it. There had been a couple of fans who hadn't gotten that the soap was a TV program and not real life. Scary. "Anyway, the number to send the fax to is 303-555-4201. And is there a charge for that? I can give you my card number."

"No. No charge. I'll cover the cost, that is if you'll send me a picture?"

"Of course. How do you want it filled out." Sometimes being something of a celebrity had some advantages.

Len managed to be in the lobby on time to meet the Croc. He had even had time to stop by the desk and pick up the fax from Indiana. Len was informed they now had a production van from the theater complex to drive out to the airport so they had to wait a short while for the driver. That gave Len time to tell the Croc what he had further learned and to hand over the fax for him to read.

"This is perfect," Croc said. "We were expecting a problem with the mother. She's a tyrant, isn't she? But with this we can make any problem with her disappear."

"I thought it might."

The driver showed up and the two of them piled into the backseat. "So what's this new girl's name?" Len asked.

"Hell, I don't know, Ruth, or Peggy. Or something. She's playing Wendy, call her that."

"That's what we do, Croc" Len sat back in the seat. "Of course, that'll make her New New Wendy won't it?"

Like most airports, Denver's meant walking long corridors to get to the right gate. They did have moving sidewalks so that made it easier. The plane from New York, by way of Houston, was on time. Len and the Croc stood back and watched while the passengers disembarked. When a travel weary blond haired slip of a girl about twenty came through the exit they went over to her. After making sure she was the right person the Croc introduced her to Len. Her name was Carol, and she looked exactly like what Wendy should look like. Very pretty, petite, fresh, sexy without being provocative. "Hello, Captain Hook," she said. And she curtsied. Cute. This girl was going to be perfect for the part.

"Nice to meet you." Len said. They shook hands.

While the driver went with her tickets for her luggage the three of them headed off toward the parking lot.

Len, while they walked, took the chance to explain to the girl why she was going into the chorus for the first week. He also sounded her out about going along with the ruse he had worked out. She was willing. "In that case, how would you feel about making yourself look different. So you aren't quite so pretty."

"Why, Captain, aren't you nice. I could do that. Maybe put my hair back? Or I could wear glasses? And no make-up. Would that be enough?"

"I think that would be just fine." So it turned out she was a good sport. "This will make the whole thing much easier to pull off, you know?"

Notes
From
Home

You might be able to get a doctor's appointment for the same day in Kansas, but that doesn't mean the doctor would be able to see you right away.

Kathy and JB sat in the reception room for several hours, watching people come in and be taken to the examination rooms before them. Kathy was being fitted in between other appointments and would have to wait her turn.

It dragged on forever. JB had to keep consoling Kathy about the ruination of her marriage, help dry her periodic tears, reassure her that she probably wasn't infected with HIV, and try to fill her in with what he, as a layman, knew about AIDS and its effects. That was quite a lot actually.

JB lived in New York, ground zero for the AIDS pandemic, and by now, six years into the disease, he had more experience with it than he wanted or needed. He had been at the bedsides of several of his friends, and had served with GMHC as a buddy to another couple of dying men. And like most gay men he kept himself updated on the disease by reading the news and published reports. JB explained what he could to her as clearly as he was able, assuring her that she would most likely be safe, until finally they both lapsed into their own silences. Kathy, JB knew, was thinking out what she had to do with the situation she now faced. JB was being more prosaic by trying to figure out the code that Vince Barkley had used in his notebooks.

He knew it was a switch code. That much he was sure of. Vince had used one letter for another. But what letters? JB could pretty well figure out the usual and most used letters, e's and i's and t's on each of the pages. So a word that used two or more e's or was only two letters was reasonably clear. He could guess that vhh was probably see or gee, or fee, and that lq was in, or on, or to, or some such.

What really confused him and made the code more difficult to figure out was each page used different letters for those repeated letters. Since there were over twenty letters in the alphabet, it led to millions of combinations Vince could have used. JB flipped through the pages of the book and finally noticed that the first thing on every page was a number. It was different on each page, but consistent in that it was there. Then it dawned on him—what if the number at the top of each page was the key? The number at the top of the page was how many alphabetic letters Vince had skipped to get to the letter used to replace the correct letter on that particular page. That meant, if the number at the top of the page was a three, that JB had to count three letters over from the correct letter in the alphabet and replace that right letter with that third letter. That would make an A a D, a J an M, and so on. It all depended on which number was at the top of the page. Perfect. It was broken. JB had the code that Vince had used.

JB flipped to the last page in Vince's notebook to spell out what Vince had written before he died. He discovered that there was a raw edge in the fold of the book there. A missing page. It was the last page Vince had written on. Taken by someone that didn't want the contents known. JB surmised it held the name of the person Vince was meeting before he met with Howard. Howard had an appointment with Vince at eleven that night out at the bridge. The notes probably indicated who was to meet Vince before Howard. That person would have been his killer.

The page before the torn one held a date for the week before Vince died. The entries on the page were started again with a three, that had been the most common number Vince used.

Under that last Thursday was:
Hgzdug. Glqqhu. Zlfklwd. 9:30SP
    That translated to:
Edward. Dinner. Wichita. 9:30PM

That was interesting. Edward, huh? Could it be Eddie? He was n't gay. Was he? Could he have been seeing Vince on the sly? What might have been going on with them? Eddie didn't appear to be gay. He'd been a huge homophobe back in high school. But JB had learned long ago that sort of attitude was often used as a cover-up for the person's real feelings. Aggression toward what you knew deep inside you really were. If that was true it put Eddie firmly on JB's suspect list.

Another entry said:

Whuub zloo ohw KI vwdc. Klwpdq duudqjhg.

Using three letters over it read:

Terry will let HF stay. Hitman arranged.

If HF was Howard Fellows, which fit, it meant that Howard had indeed been set up in the jail that night. Terry had lied. He hadn't let Howard stay in the library out of the goodness of his heart. He left Howard there so that he could be gotten to without jail bars to hinder access. Did Terry kill him? Or was there some other arrangement for him to be killed? It could have been Terry. He jumped to number one on JB's list.

Kathy came out of the doctor's rooms and JB drove her home. She told him what he already knew, that the test would take a week to get back her results. She had to live with that fear for the time it took. JB had gone through the same thing months before when he took his own test for the virus. His had come back negative . He felt she would too.

They promised to meet before JB left town, and then he drove back to the hotel. He needed to get ready for his dinner with his Mother that evening. He went up to his room, undressed, and got into the shower. The hot water felt wonderful on his back and shoulders. He felt the pounding wet heat relaxing the twisted muscles. This case was stressing him out more than he'd realized. Not to mention the loss of his galley's. One worry on top of another. He leaned forward and let the water pour over his neck.

There was a thump. Something hitting the wall outside the bathroom. What was that? Then there was another thump. Some object thrown against the bedroom wall. He turned off the water, wrapped a towel around his waist, and opened the door.

Somebody had been in the room. Some destructive someone. Drawers were pulled out and their contents left scattered on the floor. The book manuscript that had been piled on the desk was now pushed off and three-hundred eighty-seven pages were spread all over the floor. The person who'd done this wasn't to be found. The room was empty, The door was closed.

JB stepped out of the bathroom and started across the room toward the desk. As he did his still wet feet stuck to the manuscript pages that were scattered over the floor. He also felt the papers that had stuck on his feet slide on the other pages still lying about. Then his right foot slipped out from under him, he lost his balance, and he fell backwards. When he landed JB felt his ass land solidly on top of his left ankle. Hard. The ankle had bent under him and took the brunt of his full one hundred and seventy pounds. There was a searing pain as the ankle was squashed under his weight, along with a sickening sound. That was it. He'd broken or sprained something in his fall. And the pain was fricking intense. He pulled his ankle out from under him and grabbed at it with both hands. A moan escaped. He rocked back and forth as waves of pain pulsed up his leg.

As he lay there, through the pain, he also realized that the envelope that had held Howard's notes was gone. The drawer they had been in had been pulled out and tossed. The contents, the envelope, weren't anywhere around it. It had been stolen.

He heard a soft knock on the door and he tried to get up by grabbing the footboard of the bed. He gingerly put weight on the ankle he had injured. More pain shot up his leg and he went right back down to the floor. An envelope was shoved under the door. JB shouted out, "Hey. Help me. I'm hurt. Come in! Help!"

The doorknob turned. The door opened slightly, and the head of the bellboy stuck around it. He spotted JB on the floor, then came in.

"Are you all right, sir?," he asked.

"No. I've injured my ankle. I need some help."

The bellboy went to the desk, bent to the floor, and picked up the phone. "I'll call the house detective. He'll know what to do." He dialed a three digit number, spoke for a moment, and then hung up. He went back to JB. "What can I do?"

"Well, you could get me some clothes to put on. Up there, on the bed." JB had set out the slacks, shirt, and jacket he had planned to wear that night. "I have underwear in the bag there. And socks too."

The boy went over to the tipped over luggage rack and looked in the bag that was now lying open on the floor. He pulled out a pair of jockey shorts and some black socks and came back. JB pulled on the shorts and got one sock on. Then decided he didn't want to try to put on the other, not with the throbbing he was experiencing at his ankle.

"Could you help me stand and get to the bed, young man?"

The boy bent. JB slid his arm over the boy's shoulder. He stood and JB went up with him. JB hopped over to the bed and sat. Then he finished getting dressed. Even the feel of the trouser fabric sliding over his left ankle caused him intense pain. This was serious and hurt like hell. It needed to be looked at right away.

JB heard another knock on the door and a voice. "Sir. It's hotel security. I'm coming in." When he looked up George, his old friend and a cop from the local jail, stood in the doorway, wearing a suit and tie instead of his uniform. It looked like he was moonlighting as the hotel dick. JB was glad it was a familiar face at his door.

"JB? What happened?" George came in all concerned and quietly took over, and the situation was under control in moments. First, George got JB four aspirin from the cabinet in the bathroom, then sent the bellboy for a wheelchair to be brought to the room.

In less than ten minutes JB was downstairs, in George's car, and they were headed for the emergency room of the Peebels Community Hospital.

Notes From The Road

A nights sleep and Len was up early to have breakfast and to get to the theater for the morning meeting. The Denver performing complex was also in the downtown area where the hotel was so it afforded him a chance to walk over to it. One of the joys of living in New York for Len was the opportunity to walk everywhere One of that city's great pleasures in an increasingly mobile world. Not only was it good exercise—it never hurt to keep in shape Len figured—but it gave him a chance to get inside his head while he worked out solutions to his daily affairs. He especially enjoyed the walk to the Broadway theater each night as it gave him time to prepare for that evening's performance. Denver would be a good place to play he decided as he turned on Champa Street and headed for the complex.

Most of the cast members were already in the theater when he arrived. However, the Croc hadn't arrived yet so they'd gathered in small circles to ponder what was up. Len went to the craft table, fixed a cup of coffee for himself, then picked up a bear claw and headed for the first row of seats. As he got comfortable, the Countess sat down beside him.

"Well, Captain, what have you come up with on the case of our perfidious pirate?"

"Quite a bit actually. I've narrowed it down to a few suspects. Three to be exact. And the meeting today will probably work to ferret the main culprit out. It's moving along."

"What is today about, anyway? I could have used a few more hours of sleep."

"The Croc will explain when he gets here."

Which he did at that moment.

He came striding on stage with Carol under his arm. She didn't look quite the same as she had the evening before. She had done as she said she'd do. Her hair was pulled back and she wore a pair of dark framed glasses. In addition she had applied no make-up, save for a touch of lipgloss. She looked if not unattractive, then certainly what one would call plain.

The Croc clapped his hands and called for everyone's attention. First, he introduced Carol as a chorus addition for the young lady being used as New Wendy's replacement in her Princess part. He sent her over to Mike who would be her supervisor. There was some tepid applause for her, meaning the cast would reserve judgment until after a performance. The Croc then went on and dropped his more explosive announcement. He told everyone that the current Wendy was to be replaced.

That got everyone's attention.

Furthermore, he added, there would be auditions the next day for anyone in the cast who felt they could play the part. There would be a flyer on the board with the details later that day. That set the whole cast to whispering.

The Countess leaned over to Len and said, "Very clever, Captain. She'll audition, of course. But how will that catch her?"

"You'll find out on the day, my dear. Should be fun don't you think?"

The Croc went on with the rehearsal, so the cast could get used to the new stage and he could make any blocking changes that being in a different theater might require.

It was a long day of hard work. During the lunch break Len even got included in an argument between New Wendy's mother and the Croc. She was naturally upset that her daughter was being replaced. Understandable from her viewpoint, except that New Wendy herself expressed a decided *I don't care* attitude. The mother was pushing hard for New Wendy to go back to her old part as the Indian Princess, and New Wendy stated she only wanted to go back to Staten Island. Len knew the reason.

She got her wish when the director pulled out the fax copy of New Wendy's birth certificate. He threatened to charge the mother with falsifying a legal contract by lying about her daughter's age. New Wendy being presented as seventeen and really being only thirteen voided her contract. That left her mother open to substantial fines with Equity and probably charges from the Child Labor Department of New York City and possibly San Francisco too. The dragon lost its fire breathing abilities and backed down quickly. The problem was solved for all parties concerned.

Once the meeting broke up New Wendy ran to Len and threw her arms around him. "Thank you so much," she said. "I knew after I let it slip you would check it out. I get to go home because of you. Thank you. Thank you."

"You planned that? That was very sneaky, my dear. But won't you miss the business?"

"Not on your life. I only want to be a normal kid."

"Whatever that is. Well, then, farewell little one." He kissed her forehead.

A little later in the day both Nancy and Marta, either one of which could play Wendy, came to Len and started asking questions again. First they wanted to know what was expected of them.

"From what I understand," Len said. "They're going to have each of the auditioners sing any tune they want to show their vocal range. Then they'll do the lines preceding Wendy and Sneed's love song and dance in scene 9. So you need to get a song up and ready. And study the part. Is that what you wanted?"

Nancy asked, "Do you know who will be reading with us?"

"Probably Sneed. And they might ask you to do a little of the dance too. To see how you and Sneed move together. You should probably watch the number tonight. See if you can't pick up some of the choreography."

Marta said, "Can we look from the wings?"

"I don't see why not. Good luck guys."

They walked off with their heads together, excitedly discussing what the audition could mean for them. Then it dawned on Len, there were three girls who could do this part. Where was the last one? He headed toward his dressing room and, luckily, ran into her on the way.

"Gwen," he said. "Why aren't you all worked-up about this audition. You could play Wendy as well as any of those other girls."

She looked at the floor. "Do you think I could?"

"You're the right age. And you can sing. Aren't you a soprano?" She nodded.

"And you can dance?" Another nod. "Then that should be enough."

"Then I will. Thank you."

Notes
From
Home

The Community Hospital had begun as a ten bed private clinic started by Dr. Osgood Meadows back in the 1950's. By the late 1960's it had been taken over by another doctor, Doc Webb, and was being subsidized by the city. It was expanded then to thirty beds plus an emergency room, and served as the main medical facility for the fifty or so miles surrounding it.

It was in the emergency room that George and JB were sitting while JB filled out the paper work that would allow them to treat him. Raising his foot in the wheelchair he was in hadn't lessened the pain he was feeling, but he was suffering it in relative quiet. At least until a wave would crash on the shores of his brain and engulf his senses. Then he thought he might pass out. What was helping was the fact it was a weekday night, so it wouldn't take long for him to get seen.

JB signed the papers and George took them over to the nurse's station. It was less than five minutes later that a blond boy with soulful blue eyes and wearing a medical coat walked up to JB. He couldn't have been more than twenty-three and looked like he should have been starring on *Head Of The Class*, the TV sitcom.

"I'm Doctor Taylor..." JB thought he should have added a cute in there. I'm Cute Doctor Taylor. "...Are you in pain?" he asked.

"I think I have a broken ankle. You guess."

"Well, let's get you inside and take a look. I can give you something for the pain too." Young or not JB liked this very attractive young man. He went behind JB and rolled him off.

JB turned toward George and said, "Could you call my mother and tell her I'm here. She'll worry if I don't show up for our dinner date."

"Will do," George answered.

Once inside JB was driven to a table. He hopped to it and unbuckled his slacks. They slid down and pooled at his feet. He lifted himself up onto the table while the doctor pulled the pants off, handed them to JB, then bent over his foot. JB would have said something charming and teasing, except the doctor touched his foot. Instead, JB hissed at the twinge that shot up his leg and exploded behind his eyes.

"I'm not so sure about this being broken. It might be just a bad sprain" Doctor Cute said. "I'll order you some painkillers. We'll have to take X-rays to be sure." Then he walked away.

JB was left sitting in his *Calvin Klein* jockeys, with his shirttails flapping, feeling like an extra on an episode of *St. Elsewhere.*

A nurse came over after about five minutes and handed him a couple of pills. JB took them and she had him hop down and back into his chair. Then he was rolled off into the innards of the hospital. The whole thing had taken about 10 minutes. If it had been New York JB would still be waiting in the ER lobby and probably watching a knife fight between a couple of gang members while the cops tried to pull them apart. One small benefit of Kansas over the Big Apple.

Also, within another ten minutes JB was feeling fine. No more pain in his foot or anywhere else on his body. Even his dandruff didn't itch. The wonders of modern medicine. Take a pill and we all go away to Happyland, but let's not talk about the cost of the addiction that becomes the fare for the ride.

JB's ankle was X-rayed. It turned out it was a sprain. Dr. Cute than wrapped it in miles of gauze,.mixed a tub of quick-drying medical plaster and began applying it to JB's ankle. The plaster took a little more than thirty minutes to dry and weighed enough to make JB think he could have done a credible Quasimoto dragging his foot behind him up the steps of Notre Dame Cathedral. It also seemed to be a bit of overkill for a sprain. In New York one of those Velcro and fabric braces would have been more than sufficient. Next JB was given a set of wooden crutches plus more of the pain pills, and was going to be released. But he wasn't leaving the hospital.

Somewhere in between the X-rays and the cast he had found a chance to read the note that the bellboy had slipped under his door before JB had called for him. The note was from Shirley Fellows, and told him that her mother, Vivian, had been attacked by someone who had broken into their house and ransacked Howard's room. Vivian was currently being looked after in the same hospital.

Once JB was released he limped on his crutches to the elevator and went up to the second floor. The nurse stationed there directed him to Vivian's room and JB hobbled there straight away.

Shirley, in her capacity as nurse, was standing beside her bed. Vivian was sleeping. Shirley, when she saw JB, came to the doorway and indicated he should follow her. He did, to a couch stationed at the end of the hall. They sat.

"Is she all right?" JB asked

"They gave her a sedative. She was hurt pretty bad."

"What happened?"

"Mom told us that she was awakened this morning by the sound of someone in the house. She got out of bed and went to investigate. What she found was a masked man in Howard's room going through his things. She confronted him, and he attacked her. But she fought back and he ran away. She was knocked out though. And we didn't find her until I went over in the afternoon to see why she wasn't answering her phone."

"Did she get a look at the man?"

"No. She said he was wearing a mask. One of those Halloween kinds. She said he looked like Ronald Reagen."

"She must have been frightened to death. Ronnie sure as hell scares me, but that's for a whole other set of reasons"

"She probably was scared, but she was very brave too. She even tried to defend herself against the attacker. On the way to Howard's room she went into the linen closet and grabbed what she thought was a spray can of ammonia. She was going to blind him."

"I always knew she was a tough old bird. I can see her spraying at that guy."

"Well, it didn't go as she planned. She grabbed the wrong can and ended up spraying the guy with paint."

"Paint?"

"Yeah, black lacquer."

That's when the elevator doors opened and JB's Mother and George stepped out. He waved at them and they came down the hall together. Mother was in her Sunday special occasion dress. A navy blue lace number that was in fashion maybe ten or so years before. And a hat. One of those starched net things that went over her hair like a helmet and looked like a wire trash bin turned upside down, with a flat velvet bow on the top in the same dark blue as her dress.

"Well, what have you done to yourself now," JB's mother said. Always sympathetic, his mum.

"I have a sprained ankle. Nothing major. I'll be on crutches for a couple of weeks. That's all."

"Well, praise the Lord for that." She looked at Shirley. "How's Vivian?"

"We're not sure. She had a bad scare, and a concussion. And with her heart condition. We'll have to wait and see."

"Well, I guess we'd better get you back home, hadn't we, Jeremy."

"Didn't we have a dinner date?"

"Well, yes, but with this."

"I have a nice big supply of painkillers, and I'm already dressed. Except for my slacks." The Doctor had applied the cast, but had torn the leg of JB's slacks so they would fit over the bulky plaster.

His Mother looked at his foot. "I'm pretty sure your slacks can be saved. They're only torn at the seam. They can be repaired. Meanwhil, I have safety pins."

"Good. These are Ralph Lauren, and not cheap."

"You do look very nice."

"Thank you." JB had on tan slacks, a blue on blue striped shirt, a dark blue sports jacket, and a lighter blue patterned scarf that went under the coat collar and hung in front. "The jacket is Ralph Lauren too. I got it for my last book junket. The scarf was a gift from Len. He's always trying to make me dress more stylishly. You look very pretty too, Mother. Since we're all dressed there's no reason why we should miss our night out."

"Well, I'll drive then."

There was some hurried activity back at Vivian's room. A nurse ran in, followed by a doctor.

"Oh, dear," Shirley said. "I'd better go see what's happened." She was up and off to the room.

JB looked after her. "Mother, would you do me a favor."

"Of course. What?"

"Go to the nurses station and call Sara. She'll want to know what's happening here."

"Whatever for? Why would Sara need to know?"

"I just think she would, Mother. Please?"

"Well, all right," she said and left to make the call.

JB then turned to George. "Before we go to dinner, I was wondering if we could stop at the police station. Could you get me copies of some pictures."

"Sure, JB. But of who?"

"Let's see. I'll want one of Vince Barkley, Terry Rickman, Eddie Falco, Randy Sparks, Goldy from the bar, and one of Howard too. Can you do that?"

"I think I can. What do you need them for?"

"I want to show them around. See if they're recognized."

The drive over to Wichita was uneventful, except that JB's Mother went about three miles per hour all the way. "You could go a little faster, Mother. I think every car for the last twenty miles has passed us."

"The speed limit is there for a reason, Jeremy."

"Yes, but the suggested minimum isn't twenty under what's on the signs. And getting the finger from all those drivers isn't much fun."

"We'll get there on time, and safely."

Miraculously they actually weren't late for their reservation. *La Maison de Butterfly* looked like it had been built as a chain place that had gone bust, leaving the building open for a new occupant. There had been some attempt to disguise its antecedents but the bones still showed. You couldn't hide the *Kenny Rodgers Fried Chicken* background with a little frou-frou and a tassle.

There was a bar to the left as they walked in, and the restaurant stood beyond. It had been redecorated with blue printed toile wallpaper and ornate crystal and gold candleiers. Hung on the walls were gilt rococo framed Paris street scenes. At the windows were swags of yellow damask curtains held back with elaborate ties. However, the vinyl covered banquettes and Formica topped tables were completely out of place. It was as if Marie Antoinette had shopped at *Bed, Bath, and Beyond*. Wrong. Just wrong.

They were escorted to their table and the maitre d' put

down menus. Water was delivered and JB took another pill, then looked at the double fold carte du jour. It was a litany of semi-French dishes, heavy on the sauces, with translations to English in italics beside them. Julia Child would have picketed the place in a heartbeat.

JB looked around and scoped out the customers at the other tables. They were a swarm of what in New York would have been Upper East Side opera queens. All fluffed and manicured and tidily wearing narrow silk suits and shiny ascots. Does *anyone* still wear an ascot?

The waiter came up and greeted them in one of the most atrocious French accents JB had heard since Barbra Streisand had the gaul to sing an album of French songs. It was literally Moan-sewer for Monsiéur and Mercy for Merci.

"First, please drop the accent. I've heard better French in Bugs Bunny cartoons."

The waiter smiled and said, "Thank you. I keep telling the boss I don't speak French, but does he listen? What can I get you?"

"What's the chicken of the day?"

"Coq a la Milanaise." Cock ala me-lann-uh-nase is what he said.

"That will be fine. And perhaps a salad Nicosia to begin. What will you have Mother?"

"What's that your having?"

"Chicken breast dipped in egg, bread crumbs and Parmesan cheese. With a salad."

She shut the menu. "That will be fine."

"Oh, and a white to drink. A blanc de blanc perhaps?"

"Yes, sir." He left and JB looked over at his Mother. "Now, we can talk. What was it you wanted to say?"

"I think its time I said this, Jeremy. I know you'll think I shouldn't, but I do worry about you. Since you insist on living the lifestyle you've chosen."

"Mother, it isn't like it's going to change any time soon. It's been twenty years I've lived as my true self. It's a fact, not a choice. No matter what you may hope for."

"If that is the case then I suppose I must accept it."

My God, this was a huge admission for her, JB marveled. This from the woman who refused to even mention him when he first came out. She wiped out his entire existence from the whole flaming family. She had reduced him to a magician's trick.

She went on. "I accept it grudgingly I must admit. But I repeat, I worry for you. You seem so alone, son. Especially since you no longer see Len."

"Not the case at all, Mother. I see Len quite often. And I have many other friends. Not as many as I had I know, but still more than one or two. I have lost several people to this terrible disease."

"And that is another thing I worry about."

"Once again, I take very good care of myself. And I don't take chances."

"But, from what I've read it only need be one contact."

How about that? JB was thinking. He sat back in his chair. She was interested enough in his life to do some reading about AIDS. Old dogs and new tricks came to mind.

"That's true. And that's why I'm careful," JB said.

"But what if something should happen? What will you do then?"

"I have an excellent doctor in New York, Mother."

"Is that enough? What I mean to say, Jeremy, is if something should happen I want your promise that you will return here, to your home. If you become ill I want you where I can look out for you."

"In Kansas? Is that wise, Mother? What about the town's reaction?" Everyone had read about Ryan White and the Florida hometown that had ostracized him. Blatant prejudice in any of its forms is never pretty.

"Hang the town's reaction. At a time like that you should be with family. And I hope you will need your family."

JB was, to say the least, caught there with his pantaloons waving in the wind. For this woman, who even now didn't approve of his life choices, to make such an offer took a great deal for her. It turned out that for her family was the stronger bond, no matter what might try to take it asunder. Parents? Just when you think you know them they'll turn around and be caring on you.

After they ate and were deciding if dessert was called for JB took a moment to call the waiter over. He pulled out the envelope of pictures George had given him and asked, "Do any of these people look familiar to you? Have they been here before?"

"Uh, I'm sorry sir, but it is a house rule that we never discuss our patrons. You see, we tend to serve a very special clientele and they would be very upset if we identified them to everyone. I could lose my job if I did." The closet still doing its most insidious work. Why is it that even gays themselves will co-operate in perpetuating a draconian system that keeps them and other gay people hidden under rocks like lizards and horned toads?

"Well, how about if I promise to only use the information in my investigation of a crime that happened elsewhere. Would that help?" The waiter looked dubious. "And, what if I offered you remuneration for your discrete counsel?" JB held out two twenty dollar bills. Some thing's work regardless of location. Money spoke volumes in both New York and Kansas. The waiter looked in both directions then leaned down to peruse the photos.

He pointed to Vince. "He's been here a lot. With this guy most of the time." He pointed to Eddie. "They sure looked like a couple." The waiter looked at JB's mother then leaned over and whispered to JB. "Yeah?" JB said. He nodded, then put his finger on another picture. "Let's see, I've seen this one before. He uses the bar to pick up tricks." It was Howard. "And, everyone knows Goldy. Humm, I don't know him..." Randy. "...but I'd like to. And this one has been here once that I know of." That was Terry. "With this one." Vince again.

"Well, thank you." JB handed over the cash. "You've been very helpful."

When he'd left JB's mother asked, "How did that help, Jeremy?"

"It tells me who killed Vince Barkley. Now all I have to do is get him to admit it."

Notes From The Road

Later that evening, after his dinner, Len got on the phone again to contact JB. He wanted to find out what was happening with the case JB was looking into. And to tell JB about what he had found about his musical saboteur. Also it gave him a chance to gloat a little over his plan to ferret her out. He wasn't sure which of the three women was his culprit. Was it Nancy, Marta, or Gwen? All he knew for sure was it definitely was one of them.

JB told him that his case was almost finished because he had a good idea of who he was after. The next day or two would have it wrapped up neatly for him. He also told Len he was on crutches from a badly sprained n ankle. That was a shocker. And the explanation as to how and why was just as puzzling. What was in those notes that someone wanted so badly? Then JB asked Len how his case was going.

Len explained what he had so far figured out, and how he was going to catch her. "I'm not sure if it's Nancy or Marta that I suspect more. Both of them are super anxious to win the part."

"What about the other girl? What's her name?"

"Gwen. She hasn't shown any interest at all. In fact, I had to talk her into trying out tomorrow. But, I wouldn't put it past any of them."

"Have you ever read any Earl Stanley Gardner?"

"Who?"

"He wrote all the Perry Mason mysteries. You should look into them."

"Whatever for?"

"We get clues from all sorts of places. Pick one up, Len. It might help."

"I'll do that."

After their conversation Len went down to the hotel gift shop. They had a rack full of paperbacks but no Perry Mason mysteries. Then he went to the front desk and spoke with the clerk. That sent him outside the hotel and two blocks down to a local video store. Many old TV series were becoming available on VCR in the last year or so.

Len checked and, sure enough, he found a tape of two episodes from the old Raymond Burr series. He purchased the tape, and went back to his room.

He settled in for an evening of courtroom drama with Della Street and Perry Mason, although if the scuttlebutt in the industry was right about Raymond Burr it would better be Fairy Mason and Della Christopher and Gay Streets.

Len watched the episodes all the way through. They left him scratching his head. He had no idea why JB had directed him to these particular mysteries. There was supposed to be something in them that would help? Other than them being good television, Len couldn't see the point. He set the tape to rewind. Now that he knew who the killer was maybe a second watching would make what JB had in mind clearer.

The second time around Len was able to start seeing where the clues had been dropped in the stories, how Mason was able to figure out who the murderer was. But it didn't make why JB had led him to these particular stories any clearer. Len still couldn't see how any of it applied to his sabotage mystery. This was supposed to help, damn it. What was JB doing to him?

A third viewing of the tape and the actor in Len realized that the killer had fewer scenes in the dramas than any of the rest of the cast. He walked into court, got on the stand and then disappeared until Mason called him back for a re-examination and questioned him until he confessed. Interesting from a performers point of view. Actors were always interested in how many scenes and lines they had in a part. But it still didn't apply to his problem as far as Len could see.

Another viewing proved that Len was right about the last

time through. The killer character even had fewer lines than any of the other characters in both the episodes. Intriguing. But, again, how did it apply? He'd have to call JB to find out. Len checked his watch. It was late so he'd have to contact JB on another day. After watching all that TV it was way too late to call him in Kansas, besides the auditions were the next day and Len needed to get some sleep.

Notes
From
Home

Awake the next morning at seven JB wanted to talk to the Chief about the information he had got from the waiter at the Butterfly first thing.

He decided to wear the same clothes he'd had on the night before, except he put on a clean T-shirt under his jacket. A *Miami Vice* look in a Kansas backwater? Were they ready? JB figured there was no reason for him to tear up a second pair of pants to fit over his cast, and the suit coat provided padding that would help to save his pits from the rubbing of the crutches.

JB found the Chief sitting at the counter at *Woolworth's*. It was breakfast time. He sat with him and then had to explain what had happened to his foot. That got a snort of amusement out of the Chief.

Then JB launched into what he'd now figured out from looking into the whole Howard Fellows case. The interrogations, the waiter in Wichita, what he'd put together from the pieces he'd picked up all over town. "It's my opinion, Chief, that this was not a crime of passion or of the moment."

"But what about how Vince was found? That could lead to a suspicion of spur of the moment violence, couldn't it?"

"I don't think so. Regardless of the circumstances it was carried out in, Vince Barkley's death was a cold and calculated murder." JB then explained how Vince had set up a meeting with Howard that night to try to get him to stop his story about the Peebels gay sex club. Vince was going to threaten Howard with false drug charges if he wouldn't kill the story. But before he could make that threat something went wrong. Vince ended up being killed instead of the story. Then Howard was arrested because the killer had set up Rickman to be at the bridge to find him there. That was accomplished by leaving the note on Terry's locker. "...but the person who killed Vince was out at that bridge before Howard arrived. That man had the opportunity and I suspect a motive, although I'm not completely sure what that is yet."

The Chief demurred. "I have to have a motive, JB. The county attorney won't prosecute without one. I found that out on the Fellows case."

"You mean to tell me that the CA wasn't going to charge Howard with murder after all?"

"That's right. I told him we would come up with the motive, but he refused. Until I had a reason he wouldn't charge Howard with a capital crime. He was only charged with obstruction that afternoon. Howard got a fine from the judge."

"I don't believe this. Howard wasn't even in any real trouble then? Why wasn't he let go right away?"

"There was no one to process him out. The clerk had gone for the day when Howard got back from court. We were going to get to him first thing the next morning."

"So Howard died because of a secretarial absence?"

The Chief nodded. "That's why I won't do anything on this until I have the motive. You can bet on it."

"Hey, Chief, there could be a myriad of reasons. Even exposure as a gay man in a town like Peebels might have been a good enough reason for most anyone." JB ticked off his reasoning. "The killer had been to the poker club. So he'd probably been with Vince. He was seen at the restaurant in Wichita with Vince on at least one occasion. And there's the missing page from Vince's notebook. That page, I think, had the name of the person Vince was going to meet before Howard got there that night. That's why it was torn out of the book. Vince wanted Howard's article stopped, and was afraid of what was in his story notes. That's why he was meeting with Howard. To get him to put a halt to the story. Or he was going to arrest Howard on trumped up drug charges."

"But you don't know who did it, right?"

"Wrong. I have a good idea who it was that killed Vince. And he's been trying to cover it up ever since. I'll admit I don't have the motive. I haven't figured out the why of the killing yet. But I do have an idea how we can find out."

"Wait a minute. You were syupposed to be looking into why Howard was dead. Not Vince. You're off track."

"I'm not really. What I came here for was to get Howard off the murder charges I understood you were going to use against him. To do that I had to look into Vince's death. I think Vince had everything to do with Howard being killed. But he couldn't have done it."

"How's that?"

"Well, Vince was already dead himself when Howard died, Chief. But that wasn't part of the plan, I'm sure. Vince had manipulated Howard into a place where he would have had control over him. Jail was the perfect place for accomplishing that. Vince only wanted to put a stop to Howard's exposure of the gay cop club, not kill him."

"But Howard was killed and the story was stopped anyway. Death is a good way to stop a writer from writing."

"Bad reviews often do it too. But, Howard's dying was an unfortunate consequence. It wasn't Vince's plan. Vince only wanted Howard to not write his story. If Howard had been willing to do that I don't think he'd have been killed. Howard being murdered might have been an intimidation tactic gone dreadfully wrong. Knowing Howard he probably refused to stop the story and got belligerent with his killer." JB had also figured out there were some other circumstances surrounding Howard's killing not having anything to do with the gay club story, but since the cops only needed one charge to get their suspect into court. JB would supply that and keep the other quiet. There was no reason to confuse the issues. "Howard never did react well to threats. And he believed completely in his rights as a newspaper man. That's what got him killed."

"So it was a free speech issue?"

"The right of it. But Howard left his notes for the story behind. Those had to be destroyed or the whole thing could still blow up in the collective faces of the sex club members. Those notes could have ruined lives. Vince's murderer had to have them. That's why Howard's mother was attacked, and why my room was ransacked. To get the notes to Howard's story."

"But that still doesn't explain why Vince was killed."

"That's why I wanted to talk to you this morning. I think

together we can get the guy who killed Vince to confess. Or at the least, implicate himself. Wouldn't that give you enough to arrest him?"

It took the rest of the morning for the Chief and JB to get his plan worked out. When they were ready the Chief drove JB to the three-hundred block of Main Street. The street was quiet, its twenties and thirties buildings as busy as they would get on an early weekday afternoon in Peebels, Kansas. Sixteen pickup trucks in a row, parked in slantwise slots along the street. A couple of old men sprawled in their regular spots in front of the newspaper office. Two women with shopping bags in hand talking in the middle of the sidewalk. The diner full to its capacity with a lunch crowd of six endeavoring to get their food down so they could return to their jobs on time.

They parked a block away from their target and JB struggled to get out of the patrol car the Chief came around and held out his arm, helping JB to stand. "You going to be all right with this, JB? I sure don't like sending an invalid in to do this sort of thing," he said.

"It's my theory, Chief. I kinda have to follow up on it, don't I? I can't see you pulling this off. anyway. Its not at all your bag. Relax, Chief, I'll be fine."

The Chief stood next to the car watching JB as he awkwardly made his way down the block.

JB used the end of his crutch to pull open the door to the office of the Falco Travel Agency and move inside. Eddie, in shirtsleeves, was sitting at his desk, looking at a computer screen. He looked up when JB came clumping in.

"What happened, JB? How'd you get the bad leg?""

"I had a fall in my room yesterday, Eddie. I sprained my ankle when someone broke in."

"Bummer."

"Yeah, and that someone took Howard's notes for his story too."

"No kidding?"

"There's no reason to play innocent, Eddie. I know it was you. I can even understand why. You don't want your secret out there for everyonethe to gossip about, do you? You think it will ruin you."

"What? I don't know what you mean."

JB went over to Eddie's desk and sat on the edge directly in front of him.

"Come on, Eddie. You don't need to hide it from me. I found out all about you last night. And I don't care. In fact, maybe you and I could get it on? How about it?"

"What?" Eddie looked around to see if there was anyone who could hear what was being said. There wasn't. They were alone in the office. But he still wasn't going to give in so easily. His closet door was shut tight. "JB, I'm not sure I know what you're talking about?

"Eddie. I know all about what you and Vince were up to. There's a waiter over in Wichita who will swear you give a class-A blowjob. How'd you like to have a matinee with me, Eddie?"

JB reached and took hold of Eddie's hand. He pulled forward and set the hand on his thigh. Then he grabbed Eddie at the neck and pulled his head in close to his crotch. "I've got to admit I was always kind of attracted to you, Eddie. Even way back in high school. This is our chance. You and me, Eddie. But I'm a top. Are you a bottom, Eddie?" Eddie hadn't pulled his hand away.

"JB. I...I don't know what you mean."

"Eddie, come on, give it up. I found out last night at *La Maison de Butterfly* that you and Vince used to eat there regularly. And were acting like a couple of lovers. I'll bet you two were a couple, weren't you Eddie? Eddie and Vince sitting in a tree," JB said, using the child's tease. "Come on Eddie, you can tell me the truth."

Eddie's hand, still resting at JB's thigh, started to move in a circle. And he smiled. One of those *Ah shucks, you got me* kind of smiles. "All right, JB. Okay, let's you and me play some. What do you want to do?" His hand was now roaming closer to JB's crotch. "I'll play with you. Do you like kinky? I can do that."

"I'll bet you'd even wear lipstick if I asked you to. Wouldn't you? Would you wear Crafty Crimson for me, Eddie?"

"Sure. If it'll turn you on. That's what I want, JB. To turn you on." Eddie then leaned forward and his head snuggled into JB's groin. JB put his hands on the back of Eddie's head and held it there while Eddie rolled his head so he could lick at JB's zipper.

"I wondered if all that macho posing you did was a cover. Now I know it was. You're as gay as I am, aren't you, Eddie? You don't need to hide with me anymore. I'm cool with it. You know I've always been attracted to you ginger boys. And you'll

f

it the bill perfectly." JB held Eddie's head up so he was looking up at him. "Come on, let's go to the back."

Eddie nodded. "Okay. We can go back there," he said. "And you heard right. I do give great head. I'll make you blow your mind."

"Although, I am wondering. Did you and Howard ever get it on together? I get that you wanted him all the way back in high school. That's why you got him to stop hanging around with me, isn't it? So you could have him all to yourself. Now it makes sense. But you didn't need to, Eddie. Howard and I weren't lovers. You could have had him back then. All you probably had to do was ask."

Eddie shook his head.

"Did you stay friends with Howard after I left town, Eddie? No, you said you didn't, didn't you? Because of Howard coming out, right? Back in the seventies. Why didn't you come out too, Eddie? Too afraid? I'll bet you dropped Howard right then and there. You couldn't afford to be pained with Howard's queer brush, could you? Is that what happened?"

Eddie started to say something but before he could JB went on.

"That's a rotten way to treat a friend, Eddie. Dropping him because he was something you didn't want to admit you were yourself. Shame on you." JB crossed his arms. "So, when did this thing you had with Vince start up? I guess you'd have thought Vince would be all right, wouldn't you? Vince was just as closeted as you were, and kept his gay ;ife hidden the same way you did yours. So it was all right to hang with him, wasn't it? How long did you two get it on, Eddie?"

JB slipped the scarf from his coat collar, folded it in half and put the fringed ends through the loop. Then he dropped the scarf over Eddie's head. He held the ends and slid the loop up tight against Eddie's neck. He held it there.

"Is this what you and Vince were into, Eddie? Is this how you two used to play around? Were you two into scarfing?"

JB tightened the fabric a little more. Eddie's hands went to his neck and clawed at the cloth that was now choking him.

"JB, I didn't...," he croaked.

JB loosened the scarf a twist.

"Come on, Eddie. Don't lie to me. I can't stand a liar. So you ell me the truth."

He tightened the scarf again. What choice did Eddie have

but to comply? JB was strangling him and held the power to make it worse.

"For instance," JB said. "I know you were the one that attacked Mrs. Barkley. Weren't you? She sprayed her assailant with black paint. I saw that paint behind your ear, Eddie. You missed it when you tried to clean up. Then, later, you broke into my room and took Howard's story notes. That's what happened, isn't it?"

Eddie started to shake his head no. JB pulled the scarf tighter.

"I said don't lie to me, Eddie. Now, you and Vince were getting it on that night out at the bridge, weren't you? You took your asphyxiation game too far and you killed him. Why, Eddie? Why did you kill your lover?"

JB loosened the scarf. Eddie coughed and again started to deny the accusation. JB pulled the scarf tight again.

"Eddie, I'm going to keep choking you until I get the truth out of you."

JB pulled on the ends of the scarf and wound them around his wrist, making it even tighter.

"Now tell me what happened, Eddie. Why did you kill Vince?"

Eddie waved his hands at JB. He wanted to speak but the tightly wound fabric prevented him. JB unwound his wrist a turn.

Eddie's hand rubbed at his throat. "All right, JB. I was seeing Vince. We would mess around. It was Vince that was into being choked. I did it to him, sure. Because he wanted it. He made me. It turned him on. I did it because he wanted me too. But I didn't kill him, JB. I wasn't there that night. Howard was the one that killed him. Not me."

The Chief opened the door and came in the office. Eddie saw him and tried to stand. JB forced him back down into his seat.

"Eddie Falco," the Chief said. "I'm arresting you for the assault and battery of Vivian Fellows. And her murder."

JB started. "What?"

"Vivian died late last night. I was notified while I was waiting outside. Her heart gave out."

"Poor Shirley, her brother gone and now her Mom. And Eddie here involved in their murders up to his eyeballs."

The Chief stepped up and put handcuffs on Eddie. "JB's a

witness that you had that incriminating paint on you, Eddie. You'll be charged for the breaking and entering of JB's hotel room too. And you can be sure I'm going to question you about the murder of Vince Barkley." He pulled Eddie to a standing position.

"But I didn't do it," Eddie protested. "I told JB that I didn't. A second ago…"

JB held up a walkie-talkie he had hidden in his coat pocket. "He heard you, Eddie. But you also admitted to being Vince's boyfriend. That would make you at the laest an accessory in Howard's death. You'll want to question him about that too, right Chief?"

"You bet. Come on, Eddie." The Chief took him by the arm and guided him out to his patrol car.

A couple of hours later George knocked on the interrogation room door at the police station. Then he opened it. "Chief, we got it," he said.

JB went past George on his crutches and made his way to the table where the Chief and Eddie were sitting. The Chief said, "What did you find?"

George put the envelope containing Howard's notes on the table. "They were in his desk drawer, Chief. I guess he hadn't got around to destroying them yet."

JB said, "That will implicate Eddie in my room robbery and the beating death of Mrs. Fellows. What will that get him? About fifteen to life, I expect. And then there's this." JB held out the plastic garbage bag he had brought in with him. "This will get him the jackpot. The hangman's noose."

JB turned over the bag and dumped the contents onto the table. Out of it came a sports shirt, a pair of jeans, and a hardly worn pair of *Reebok* tennis shoes. Eddie slumped down in his chair.

"George and I found this bag in the back of Eddie's closet." JB turned to look at him. "You should have known the closet wasn't a good place to hide anything, Eddie. Look how you've been dragged out of yours. Hiding this stuff in there couldn't save you."

"You searched my place?"

"We had a warrant, Eddie. The judge was quite willing to

sign it when we told him what we suspected." JB turned back to the Chief. "These things will put the lie to Eddie's claim he wasn't out at the bridge. The shoes have dried mud in the bottom treads. When you check you'll find it matches the dirt out there. What I can't figure is why he kept them. Why didn't you get rid of this stuff, Eddie?"

"They're brand new."

"What? The tennis shoes?" JB picked up one of them. "Make's sense, I suppose. At over a hundred dollars a pair you don't just toss them, right?" The shoe clumped back on the table; bits of dried mud scattered across the surface. JB put both his hands on the table top and leaned down to look directly into Eddie's face. "But with that incriminating mud on the bottoms? You should have at least cleaned them, Eddie."

Eddie tried a bluff. "That doesn't prove anything. I could have been out there any time."

JB pulled a slip of paper from his coat pocket and waved it under Eddie's nose. "But this piece of Vince's notebook that I found in the shirt pocket puts you right in the middle of this, Eddie. You tore it out that night, didn't you? You knew Vince kept notes on what he did. You couldn't let this be found."

"That note is only a bunch of jumbled letters. It doesn't mean anything."

"Eddie, you dummy. It's a code. Vince knew what it said. And after I broke his code I know what it says too."

JB handed the note page over to the Chief. "I translated it. The third item on the back of the page says, 'Meeting Edward. Get it on. Work out problem-re: Howard.' That was at ten o'clock the night Vince was killed, Chief. Well before Howard arrived at eleven."

JB sat down at the table and turned to Eddie. "You've been caught dead to rights. You may as well tell us. What was the problem that you and Vince were going to work out? And how was Howard involved?"

Eddie was defeated. He knew he was in real trouble and no amount of bluff or lying or denial would help. He sat forward in his chair and leaned on the table.

"Vince was going to have Howard hurt real bad if he didn't stop the story. I didn't like it. I knew what Howard was like. He wouldn't have given up writing his story. He was real stubborn like that. Vince had bullied everybody in town long enough anyway. We were all sick of it. Vince wouldn't see that there might be a better way to stop Howard. I figured that if Vince wasn't around then he couldn't do anything to Howard."

"But you were wrong."

"I didn't know that Vince had already set Howard up. Vince had already arranged for someone in the jail to wait for Howard to show up there. I really didn't want Howard hurt. Don't you get it?"

"Of course I do, Eddie. I loved him too. You still carried a torch for him, didn't you? Even after twenty years."

That got to him. Eddie broke down. "I'm sorry. I'm so sorry for all of it. I'm so sorry."

"Right, Eddie, that really helps. I'll pass that on to Howards' sister. And his mother too. Oh, that's right. I can't. Because she's dead."

"They wasn't supposed to die. Vince didn't want that. I didn't either. She was an accident..."

"Correct, Eddie. Vince didn't." JB turned to the Chief. "Vince's plan was outlined on the other side of that page. Howard wasn't supposed to be killed. Only threatened."

"Then what happened?" the Chief asked.

"I think that there was a argument in the jail. Howard's killer got dangerously out of control and killed him. By strangulation."

"Then who?"

"Oh, that was Randy, of course. If you check the pink web belt he wears against the bruises on Howard's neck I'm sure that they'll match. So, that would make it manslaughter on his part, right? Since it wasn't pre-meditated? Then Randy went back to the cell, grabbed the sheet off Howard's bunk, and hung him in the jail library. That would be obstruction."

"But how could he?"

"With some help. From Terry Rickman probably. He was the policeman on duty that night, wasn't he?" The Chief nodded. "Then Terry let Randy have free run that night so he could get to Howard. Vince must have bullied Terry into letting Randy do that. That make's Terry an accessory too?"

The Chief wasn't a happy man. He finally knew the amount of corruption that ran throughout his department. There was a cleanup on the horizon. And Terry the first recipient of its sweep.

"Then that wraps it up," JB said. "Except Eddie didn't have my galleys. I looked for them. Where the hell are they?"

Notes From The Road

The anticipation for the auditions had grown among the company until that day the seats in the theater held well over half of the cast. The rest of them were at the craft table on stage scarfing up the coffee and doughnuts that had been supplied.

Nancy, Marta and Gwen were huddled together over on the other side of the stage, and the Croc was standing with the piano player over on stage right. A microphone had been set up at the center facing a table next to the piano. Since musical stage actors were almost always miked these days it wasn't necessary for them to project in the way Len had been made to do when he started out. Much easier on the throat, and it gave the players a chance to give a subtler performance.

As the starting time approached there was a disturbance over with the three women. Nancy was holding her stomach and bending over. Looking pale and queasy she got up and ran toward backstage. Presumably for a bathroom. Nervous actors?

Len went over and asked if there was anything wrong.

Marta said, "Nancy was complaining that she felt sick. That's why she had to run off stage. As a matter of fact," she added, "I don't feel all that great myself."

"Maybe you want to skip the audition?" Len asked."

"No, I'll still do it."

"Good, girl."

Len went over and sat next to the Croc at his table. He leaned in and explained. "Then let's get on with it," the Croc said. He sat forward on his chair and made a note on the yellow pad in front of him. "Go ahead, Marta. Give your music to the accompanist."

She handed over the sheet music and went to stand in front of the mike. He played an arpeggio, and she started to sing the first notes of *What I Did For Love* from *A Chorus Line*. She didn't do enough, unfortunately. Her voice wavered and she missed one of the upper notes. Then before she was to the bridge she stopped. "I'm sorry. I'm so nauseous I can't sing. I'm really sorry."

The Croc looked up from his pad. "That's all right, dear. You did enough to get an idea. And we know your abilities. Thank you. Maybe you should rest?" The Croc dismissed her. She nodded sadly, and still holding her stomach, left the stage.

"Gwen, you're next. What are you going to sing?"

She handed over her music and spoke quickly to the piano player. "I'll do *I Believe In You* from *How To Succeed*." It was an old show tune that had made a minor mark on the pop charts for Michelle Lee. Gwen stood tall and sang with gusto. Her soprano wasn't taxed by the song, but it managed to show she had a good lower range. No real lilting high notes though.

Then Sneed stood with her and handed her the sides for Wendy in the scene that led up to them singing their love song. She wasn't sure of the lines, but had a real grip on what was required by the action. She read quite well but didn't seem as sweet as the part would call for. She was a little too bawdy and knowing. After the lines the piano player segued into the song and Sneed did a waltz with her. She seemed heavy and slow when light and graceful was called for.

Finally the Croc called a halt. She looked at him hopefully, and said, "I'm sure with some rehearsal I could make the dance much better."

The Croc made a note on his pad and thanked her without making a commitment. Gwen went back to her seat at stage left and started gathering her things. That's when Carol, or New New Wendy, appeared from the back of the theater. She made her way down the aisle and came up onto the stage. "I'm so sorry I'm late," she said, exactly according to the script Len had discussed with her. "May I still have a chance to audition?"

Carol was now looking much better than her first entrance a few days before. She had let her hair loose so it fell as a shiny circle of waves around her face. Sans glasses she had applied a light make-up that enhanced her features, especially the sparkling blue eyes. She wore a charming little flowered dress over a white blouse that could have come directly from Wendy's closet.

"Of course. Give your music to the man over there," the Croc said. Gwen, ready to leave a moment before, sat heavily back on her chair.

Carol went to the mike. "I'll do *Goodnight My Someone* from *Music Man*. Okay?" And she smiled sweetly. There was that cuteness that Len had seen at the airport showing itself again.

Carol grabbed the onlookers from the very first note she sang. Her soprano was so clear and bell like the cast as audience leaned forward in their seats. Her vocal abilities clearly enchanted them. She went on to carol each sweet note precisely. As the last notes approached she gathered air and sailed easily up to the high finish. The entire cast burst into applause as she hit the soaring last note.

Sneed ran to her and hugged her. He handed her the sides and geared up to read their scene. She asked for a moment to prepare and turned away. A moment later she turned back and said her first line. The change was astounding. She wasn't a twenty year old young woman anymore. She was a fourteen year old young girl having her first crush and Sneed was the object of that affection.

When the piano took up the music she slid lightly into Sneed's arms and they glided around the stage in a smooth and graceful waltz. Then she stopped, held Sneed's arm above her, and using him as balance she performed a ballet pirouette ending with a dip to the floor as she touched her toe.

"NOOOOO!!!!"

Everything stopped while everyone looked for who had shouted. Gwen was standing and pointing at Carol, her face twisted with absolute malice. Her pointed finger shook as she took a step forward toward Carol. "You can't do this. You can't have my part. I won't let you!" Her voice was strained as she shouted. She started to rush toward Carol.

Carol, rightfully afraid, sought shelter in Sneed's arms while Len got up from the table and went to stop Gwen. He grabbed her shoulders and held her still. "Now, Gwen, you can't. If you were the better Wendy then you'd get the part. If not, then you won't. That's show business."

"But, I worked so hard. I did everything for this part. I have to have it."

"What did you do, Gwen? What was the *everything* you did to make sure you would have it? You were the one that cut the gangplank, weren't you? You made those two girls sick too? What do you have in that bag of yours?"

Len reached down and opened her tote. Inside was a giant size half empty bottle of over the counter eyedrops. "You put this in Nancy's and Marta's coffee this morning, didn't you? So you would have a clear field for your own audition. I've seen cocktail waitresses use this on unruly customers. Were you ever a cocktail waitress, Gwen?"

Gwen, by then, was leaning on Len's chest and sobbing uncontrollably. Her tears made her answering Len's questions difficult but a nod of her head confirmed what he had accused her of.

It had been Gwen who had instigated hurting the girl playing the original Wendy, the part she wanted so desperately. She had gone so far as to cause damage to the poor girl, the girl she considered an obstacle to the part she craved. Simple accidents had escalated to major hurts.

It looked as if JB had been right once again. Like all the Perry Mason stories it was the one person that seemed the least likely to have done the crime who had actually done it.

Notes From Home

The next morning JB was at the hotel lobby desk preparing to check out. Kathy Rickman stood beside him. She had volunteered to take JB to Wichita and the airport. His Mother was expected to arrive at any moment to ride along. Sara and Shirley were also expected to come and say good-bye.

JB used his credit card to pay and then the bellhop grabbed his bag to take it outside. Kathy said she would drive around to the front and pick him up, that way he wouldn't have to walk so far. Being on crutches was creating all kinds of problems for him. The sore armpits, the aching muscles in his leg from hauling around the two pound cast, and the bother of the thing getting in everyone's way.

JB started across the lobby Just then his Mother came through the revolving door. She walked straight over to him and held out a manila envelope. "Your galleys, Jeremy."

"You had them?"

"Of course. I had that nice boy over there let me in yourr room." She pointed to Corey who was standing behind the desk. "He very sweetly gave me a key. He was one of my better students a few years ago. I knew you would be far too busy with the matter of Howard's death, so I took them. I decided I would correct them. I wasn't an English teacher for twenty-five years for nothing. This way you won't miss your deadline."

"Mother, you could have left a note. I had no idea where they had got off too."

"But I did. Didn't I?"

JB shook his head.

"Oh dear. It must have slipped my mind."

"Like a penguin on a banana peel."

She sniffed. "A few less metaphor's like that in your manuscript would have been most welcome, Jeremy." She held out the twenty-seven page thick stack of his galleys snug in their envelope.

"Listen, you bitch, I won't let you do this to me!" That had come from over by the front door. Shouted out for eveyone to hear.

"Now Terry, you don't want to make a scene. Not here."

An altercation was in progress over by the revolving door of the hotel. Public screaming matches will usually draw a crowd. This was no exception. The entire lobby had stopped in their tracks and turned to eavesdrop on Terry and Kathy Rickman. They were now in the midst of what looked to be the beginning of a knockdown and drag-out argument. How embarrassing for Kathy. How uncomfortable for everyone else. Terry's hands were flying around. Kathy had her tucked under her armpits and was standing defiant in the face of his tirade.

"Oh, dear," Mother said. "Will she be all right?"

"Probably. She's a tough one when she has to be. She told me she had kicked Terry out of the house last night. Along with his getting fired from the police force yesterday and her asking for a divorce last night, I imagine he's not a happy camper today." JB turned back toward the desk and signaled Corey. He grabbed the phone to call the police.

Kathy turned on her heel and pushed out the door. Terry was left standing in place, glaring at the empty spot where she had stood. He looked around and realized that he had become that afternoon's soap opera for the entire town. *As The Stomach Turns* Live. If JB had been in the situation he might have slunk away to lick his wounds like an old hound dog. Instead Terry looked for another target. He focused on JB. He'd spotted him standing in the middle of the lobby behind his Mother.

Terry reached into his pocket and pulled out a prodigious looking spring operated switchblade knife. JB heard the blade snap into place all the way across the lobby. Terry started toward him, the expression on his face saying exactly what he had in mind. JB was the one to blame for the disaster his life had become. It couldn't be that he had aided in a murder and cheated on his wife. It couldn't be him. It had to someone else. JB was as likely as the next guy. Terry needed someplace to aim his anger.

The people in the lobby gasped and stepped away from this crazy person stomping toward JB. Terry was beyond lucid thinking and had flipped over to plain old squirrelly. As he moved toward JB, he was little more than a maniacal blitzkrieg machine. His focus was targeted at JB, and only JB. The people surrounding Terry in the lobby had vanished into the murky haze of his anger. JB was the man who was the cause of his life falling apart, and he was determined to take some kind of revenge.

As Terry passed by JB's mother she tightly gripped the envelope of galleys she was still holding, reared back, and swung them at Terry's head. She connected with a mighty blow that caused him to stumble a few steps forward. He grabbed at his head. "Ooww! Jesus!" he yelled. The knife fell from his hand and landed softly on the carpeted floor. JB's mother stepped forward at the same time and began to pummel Terry with the galleys. She shouted, "You don't attack my boy, you cheating bastard!" She rained blow after blow, one after the other, onto his head and shoulders.

JB was balancing on his crutches a foot or so in front of Terry. He shifted his weight onto his good leg, pulled a crutch from under his arm, and using it as a weapon swung it at Terry's stomach. He connected. Hard. Terry bent over, his breath taken away. A second blow with the crutch hit across Terry's shins. That took him down.

Then JB used his crutch to knock the knife away from where Terry lay writhing on the floor. It slid over the carpet and stopped safely under a table. Then JB got in a couple of pokes while his Mother continued to beat on Terry with the galleys.

By the time the Chief showed up Terry was reduced to a crumpled moaning churl lying in a ball on the flowered field of the carpet underneath him. Standing over him, ready to attack again, like a rattler striking a desert rat, was JB's mother. JB had his crutch back under his arm and was trying to look as if he hadn't participated. The awe he had at his mothers attack made it hard. Terry wasn't a threat to him or anyone else. Not anymore. It had really been an unfair fight. The two of them,

JB and his mother, against Terry. But the lobby had burst into applause when Terry went down for the count.

"Hey, hey," the Chief shouted. "Don't kill him before I can arrest him." He stood in front of JB's mother and held his hand's up.

"He was going to attack my boy, Chief. No one hurts my family. His knife is over there." She pointed to the table where JB had knocked it. "Under there."

The Chief went over and picked up the weapon. The ten inch blade flashed in the light. He folded it closed and put it in his pocket. Then he came back over to them. "Good God." The Chief shook his head.

"Chief," JB said. "You have to admit, this is one time that words really were mightier than his sword. At least as long as the word was being swung around by my Mother."

The Chief grabbed Terry by the scruff of his neck and hauled him up to a standing position. "Terry, you are a complete idiot. And you're under arrest." The Chief walked him toward the back door of the hotel. When he got to the door he didn't have to open it as Sara and Shirley had entered and held it open for him. He pushed past them and they came on into the lobby and up to JB and his mother.

"What's going on?" Sara asked.

"Comeuppance for Howard's dying. Terry was an accessory to it and the Chief was going to let him get away with only leaving the force. But Terry went all wonky this morning and has now been arrested for assault."

Shirley said, "If its some sort of revenge for Howard I'm all for it. Howard didn't deserve what happened to him."

"True. Shirley, you know, I'm really sorry this has been so hard for you And about Vivian. Eddie will be charged with second degree murder for the beating he gave her. I can guarantee you that his parole officer hasn't even been born yet."

Shirley nodded. "Poor Mom. Her heart couldn't take the trauma. It wasn't a surprise.She'd suffered for so long."

Sara took her mother's hand. "Mother, I need to talk to you. Can we sit?"

"Now? We have to say good-bye to Jeremy right now. Can't it wait?"

"No, Mother. JB is a part of it. He'll want to hear what I have to say too."

Mother sat on the chair and looked up. "Very well, what is

¡t that can't wait."

"Mom, do you remember when you told me that the most valuable gift we as human beings have been given is the capacity to love and receive love in return?"

"Yes, of course. And I also said that it was the hardest to find and the dearest to keep. That is what I believe."

"Okay, good. And do you also remember how you reacted to JB's admitting he was gay?"

"Yes. And I'm sorry for that." She turned to JB. "I want you to know that. I truly regret it."

JB smiled. "It was a long time ago, Mother. And I think there might be a chance to redeem yourself."

She looked at him quizzically, then turned back to look at Sara. Then at Shirley. Then at Sara again. She pointed and her finger went back and forth between them. "You? And Shirley?"

Sara reached out and found Shirley's hand, then smiled at her mother. Mother's hand went to her mouth as her eyes went wide.

Sara said, "Mom, I hope you'll be happy for us. Will you?" Mother didn't say anything for the moment.

JB added, "Mother, they've found love in a world that devalues what two of our kind can feel for each other. This is something to be happy about."

Mother stood and used her hands to straightened her skirt. "Of course it is. My girl is in love." She held out her arms and gathered both Sara and Shirley into them. "I am so glad for you, my dears." She kissed their cheeks and stood back. Her head turned to JB. "Is that what you wanted, Jeremy?"

"Its all any of us want, Mother. Acceptance means everything to us. Especially now, with death facing us daily."

"Because of the AIDS?"

"Of course. And there's a lack of compassion that is making this even harder. I've seen men lying totally ignored in hospitals because the staff is too afraid to go into their rooms. Its disgraceful. And certainly not what any oath they took would want them to do."

Shirley nodded her head. "I've seen it too. Not here in Peebels. We haven't had any cases, so far, but over in Wichita. There are men starting to show up at the clinics. And they're treated so badly. I wish there was something to be done."

JB said, "Maybe there is. I have something for you..." He reached into the briefcase hanging from his shoulder and pulled out the envelope of Howard's notes. "I wanted to return these to you." He handed them over. "Also, Shirley, there's a key in there. Howard got it from Randy in jail. If you take it over to Molly Sharp's place, and ask for the bag her brother left there, I think you might find a substantial surprise in it. You maybe could do amazing things with it." Shirley looked questionably at JB. "It was the real reason Randy killed Howard. He didn't want to share the money he'd stolen from that drug gang. It was a convenience for him that Vince had ordered him to confront Howard about the sex club story. Randy really wanted his key to the cache of money back. The key in that envelope that Howard had given to me. I had it, so Howard couldn't give it back even if he had wanted too. Randy and Howard must have argued and at some point Randy went ballistic. And Howard suffered the consequences. But now that Randy's facing the death penalty what you find in the bag that key opens might end up doing some good."

PRESS RELEASE

To: Peebels Daily News, Wichita Press, Topeka Journal, and other news sources.
For Immediate Release
Contact: Sara Bent
            (316) 555-2367

PEEBLES KANSAS TO BE LOCATION FOR HOWARD FELLOWS HOSPICE FOR PERSONS WITH AIDS

Three residents of the Kansas town of Peebles, located eighty-five miles outside Wichita, have banded together to create and open the Howard Fellows Free Hospice, a non-profit organization dedicated to people suffering from AIDS

A formerly private residence the newly converted Victorian mansion will serve as the location for the medical facility. Peebles residents have been at work for the last two months to make this radical change to the structure. What once was an eighteen room home built in 1887 has been renovated to become a twenty bed hospice with gardens, recreation rooms, and full time nursing care. Dr. Brent Taylor of the local Community Hospital attends. Nursing care is supervised by Shirley Fellows, RN.

The ladies, Shirley Fellows, a RN, Sara Bent, business manager of the hospice, along with Ms. Molly Sharp, a citizen, have opened the hospice with funds donated from various sources, including donations, fund raisers, and gifts.

Ms. Sharp, appointed liaison to the community, has joined the two women in giving their time, effort, and financial aid to this endeavor. Construction work has been organized by her from her many acquaintances in the surrounding area. "The workers have all generously donated their time. It has been entirely volunteer work by the men of this town," she said. Building supplies were donated from the local hardware store.

Ms. Bent stated "Two of the partners in this effort, as open lesbians, feel we have a duty to serve our fellow gay comrads in this time of crises. Molly, our other partner, simply has a giving and caring heart for those that suffer from this disease that is striking the gay community. The need for this facility was brought to our attention by my brother Jeremy Bent. He told us of patients languishing in hospitals without care or services or comforts because of fear of AIDS by hospital personnel. It is our duty to step up and help these men."

Mr. Jeremy Bent the novelist and the actor Len Matthews will be lending their names and serving as co-celebrity spokesperson's for the hospice. Mr. Bent in a statement has said, "It is an honor to support this excellent and worthy effort by these exceptional women. They make me proud to be gay and any help I can give is not nearly enough." "Ditto." was added by Mr. Matthews.

Affiliated with Wichita's St. Joseph's Hospital the hospice has, in only this first month, provided bed and comfort for three sufferer's of the disease, AIDS, which has, so far, claimed over 20,000 victims in the United States alone.

We congratulate these splendid woman for their caring and generous contribution to Peebels and the people it serves.

# # #

About the author

Ken Lansdowne has lived in California, Nevada, New York City, New Mexico, and now lives in Denver Colorado.

The first novel in *The Bent Mystery* series is *Secrets Don't Belong In Closets*, the beginning. Second is *A Murderous Ball of Fluff. The Fairy Dust Killer* is the third. Fourth is *Home Sweet HoMo.* Fifth is *Dance:Ten Murder:Maybe?* Sixth is *A Mystery, Wrapped In A Mystery, Surrounded By A Mystery.* Seventh is *The Art Of Death,* and number eight is *Bathhouse Bloodbath!*

There is also a Gay themed Christmas novella: *Jacob Marley*

If you would like to get an automatic e-mail when the next book in the series is ready for release sign up at k.lansd@outlook.com. Simply put the word "LIST" in the subject line of your email. Your e-mail address will never be shared and you can unsubscribe at any time.

Word-of-mouth is crucial for any author to succeed. If you enjoyed the book please consider leaving an online review, even if it is only a line or two: it would make all the difference and would be very much appreciated. If you didn't like it I apologize for taking up your time: my purpose was only to entertain or give you a laugh or two.